Full Circle

FULL CIRCLE

Frederick Yamusangie

iUniverse, Inc.
New York Lincoln Shanghai

Full Circle

All Rights Reserved © 2003 by Frederick Yamusangie

No part of this book may be reproduced or transmitted in any form or by any means, graphic, electronic, or mechanical, including photocopying, recording, taping, or by any information storage retrieval system, without the written permission of the publisher.

iUniverse, Inc.

For information address:
iUniverse, Inc.
2021 Pine Lake Road, Suite 100
Lincoln, NE 68512
www.iuniverse.com

Published in association with Diadem Books, Spean Bridge PH34 4EA UK
www.diadembooks.com

While the author has used real names and place names, the characters are purely imaginary.
This is a work of fiction.

ISBN: 0-595-28294-6

Printed in the United States of America

I would like to dedicate this book to
My mother:

Madam Agnes Balenga Yamusangie
(My best friend)

And also in memory of
My father:

Joseph M. Yamusangie
(My role model)

"I don't want to bother you much with what happened to me personally," he began, showing in this remark the weakness of many tellers of tales who seem so often unaware of what their audience would best like to hear. "Yet to understand the effect of it on me you ought to know how I got out there, what I saw, how I went...to the place...It was...the culminating point of my experience. It seemed somehow to throw a kind of light on everything about me—and into my thoughts. It was sombre enough, too—and pitiful—not extraordinary in any way—not very clear. And yet it seemed to throw a kind of light."

—Joseph Conrad, *Heart of Darkness*

Acknowledgements

Due to the seemingly endless obstacles, apparent and real, that I was subjected to while writing this novel, I would like to thank those who directly or indirectly gave me a helping hand:

Firstly, my heartfelt thanks are due to my mother for her guidance, understanding, patience, and teaching *(for she has been my first teacher)* and also for just being my mother *(I must be blessed to have her as my mother and I hope she enjoys this book)*.

I would also like to thank the entire Yamusangie family: thanks for your support and real friendship, Prescilia, Cynthia and Leticia, Emy and Blanchard Yamusangie; Jean-Jean Lumande; Frederick Mongeme and Frederick Muyulu; Chellie Howlett and Donna Fallows; Kashala Npenge, Peter Ngufur Jn. and Winifred Ayo; Bob Mead; Hugh Blackman; Valerie Lewsey, Peter Pascoat, Mick Nash and all the members of Thurrock Writers' Circle; all the staff of Thurrock Library at Grays *(Essex)*; Jose and Poliment Togomo.

I would like to give a special Thanks to my big sister Clarisse Yamusangie Mbuyi for her moral support, and also my cousin Evariste Kankolongo Lwaba for his advice.

I would be ungrateful if I failed to thank the staff of Woolwich Bank at Grays High Street in Essex for their outstanding customer services, especially Lucy Pree for her good financial advice *(thank you very much, Lucy)*.

And also, a special thanks to my editor, Charles Muller.

Chapter 1

▼

"C'EST L'ARRIVEE," someone said. These were the first words the boy heard when the lorry on which he and the others had been travelling at last turned into the parking lodge at Bulungu, their final destination after a two-day journey from Kinshasa. The boy was impatient to find out more about this place, which might soon become his permanent home. With his little brain he had imagined that people everywhere lived like the people at his birthplace.

The idea of clashes or differences between cultures didn't make sense to him. For him, everybody, everywhere, had the same family structures, the same moral values, the same needs—the vision of different cultures was elusive if not beyond his grasp.

Living in a house with no electricity was inconceivable to him and synonymous with death. A big-town boy, born and raised in the upper class, with little knowledge of the countryside, he had difficulty believing he could survive in this small place so far away from his parents. He thought of it as a small village. No cars, no electricity, no friends or family—to him it was indeed synonymous with death!

Bulungu was not a small village as the boy had thought, but a small town. He belonged to the elite and privileged of the regime, but now found himself in the real world. He had more knowledge of Western Europe than his own country. This was the first time he had left his home and not gone to the airport to board a plane bound for a major European city—for Brussels, Paris, Toulouse, Zurich, Geneva or Rome. His privileged background had made him more aware of the European way of life than his own.

It was around midday that the lorry that transported them entered the Bulungu parking lodge, called 'Barriere' by the local people. The boy was surprised to see a lot of people had come to welcome them. Barriere was not just a parking lodge. It was also a gathering place for the people of Bulungu—a place where everyone would come to hear the latest gossip from Kinshasa, especially regarding popular musicians. This is where one would find people who had just arrived with fresh news

The parking was on Bulungu's main high street, nicknamed *nzila ya mukili* ('road of the world') because of the belief that in this road one could practically meet anyone. It was next to the Police Station, which itself was situated at the right side of Bulungu's main market.

The boy was the star of the day. His guardian, who would soon play the role of his father, was a well-known figure and a respectable man in the town. He was a headmaster at one of the Protestant High Schools.

While the people who had come to welcome the boy were talking to each other, a man stepped out and stood in front of the boy and his guardian and said, "Good morning, Mr. Masa-Ndombe, how was the journey? How is Kinshasa?" And he added: "My people and I are very happy to see the little boy that you were talking about."

"I am also happy to see all of you," said Mr. Masa.

After listening to Mr. Masa's reply, the man looked at the boy and said, "Good morning, son. What is your name?"

"My name is…"

"Emanuel!" interrupted his guardian. "His name is Emanuel."

"Oh…you have the same Christian name as my sixth son!" exclaimed a woman from the crowd. "I think they will get on very well!"

Then some other men and women started to ask the boy similar questions. As part of the local custom the residents always put many personal questions to the visitor to make him or her feel at home—to foster a sense of belonging to the community. They believed that visitors and foreigners should always be given a warm reception and be treated well during their stay. Many residents went so far as to have especially nice dinner plates and drinking glasses or cups, not for themselves to use but to be used by any visitor or anyone passing by who may be thirsty and may need water to drink. And when anyone came unexpectedly to see them at dinnertime, they would always have a very impressive dinner set to offer the self-invited guest.

Anyone who was in the Barriere when the boy and his guardian arrived at Bulungu would have seen the local residents who came to welcome him, and seen how they expressed their hospitality to the boy who, somewhat bewildered, could barely take in what was happening to him. Surely he was in dreamland! In his short life he had never imagined he would attract so many people at once. He always thought that to become a star overnight was impossible. Famous people were only those you saw on television! In normal circumstances it would have to be his birthday for him to attract so much attention, or the beginning of July, and only then if he got good results at school. But this day didn't coincide with either of these, for it was the beginning of October.

It all seemed so unreal. The sense of being in dreamland persisted. While trying to come to terms with what was happening, he plunged into a state where he couldn't tell what was happening or hear what the people were saying about him; at the same time he saw himself in many different places at once.

After a short time, while pleasantly immersed in his self-chosen dream, his thoughts were scattered by a woman's voice. It was as though an electric shock had sparked across his tiny heart! He almost jumped out of his body when he realised that an old woman was standing in front of him and saying something to him. He struggled to bring himself back to the real world and focus on what the old woman was saying. He wasn't sure if she had asked him about his views regarding the welcome, or asked him his age, or if she was just making statements.

He didn't want to look stupid by giving a totally inappropriate answer; and by asking the old woman to repeat what she had just said might have seemed like a lack of attention, which in turn might be interpreted as a disrespectful act to the old woman. So, he just kept quiet and said nothing.

Mr. Masa, realising what was happening, came to the boy's rescue. "His name is Emanuel," he said.

"Ah…. I see," the old woman nodded.

"The boy is shy," explained his guardian.

"Shy! Why?" replied the old woman, still looking at the boy.

"Well, I wish I knew," smiled Mr. Masa.

"He shouldn't be," added the old woman. "From now on, this is his family."

Mr. Masa continued: "His real name is Dada Tshienda. Emanuel is his Christian name, but he doesn't know about it. You could see by his face how surprised he was when I said that name for the first time."

"Euh!" said someone in the crowd. "Is he from Kasai Province?"

"Yes, he is," confirmed Mr. Masa.

"It doesn't matter for now," said the same old woman who had spoken to the boy before. "He is just a boy. He is not one of those Baluba that you would, by mistake, allow into your lorry en-route from Tshikapa to Kinshasa or from Kinshasa to Tshikapa. They will definitely do you harm or even kill you just because you are not Muluba, and especially if you are Mukongo. They think of us as sub-humans. But this is just an innocent boy. He should not be confused with those murderers. Anyway, he looks like someone who was born in Kinshasa, so he wouldn't know anything about those practices."

She looked again at the boy, then raised her right hand and placed it on his head. "You are welcome in our big family, and from now on you are considered as one of our sons and grandsons. Let the spirits of our ancestors protect you from the evil work."

"Thanks, mum," said Mr. Masa.

For various reasons everybody was not able to accompany Mr. Masa and the boy to his house. It's a custom for most Bantus to welcome a total stranger with some rituals or traditional practices, especially in this case. But in Dada's circumstance, the people who were available to welcome him were from different tribes, and they came from totally different villages before settling in Bulungu. Some rituals of one may not be acceptable to others. In this small town human relationships were always taken seriously.

One of the good things about this town was that the inhabitants were willing to compromise for the sake of harmony. It was crucial that everyone was ready to compromise, which helped to preserve mutual respect and conserve harmony in their society, especially among the elders. Most of the young people, who were born there, were, in certain ways developing their own culture, based on respect for old people; but this also has its own dark side. That was something many of the elder visitors failed to notice. Older people do not believe that it exists. You need to be a young person to see it first hand. In this town older people had the habit of not taking the children's remarks seriously. Sometimes they might just pretend it does not exist, as long as it does not compromise the status of privilege they enjoy or question their authority.

On anyone's first day in Bulungu, the first thing one noticed was that the people who live there come from different cultural backgrounds and that they live in peace. But no one could easily detect the rivalry among young people. The disputes between Catholic and Protestant pupils were officially non-existent, and adults did not talk openly about the frictions between kids from different quarters. In this town, when anyone talked about the inhabitants, they actually meant the old people. So, as long the old people got along, Bulungu was a safe place to live. That was the official line. The inhabitants of Bulungu always made sure that they agreed upon the basics of people's needs.

Age was a very important factor in this town. Old people were treated with extreme respect. Anyone's parents were everybody's parents. Any parent had the right, under the sun, to discipline anyone's child. The education of any child was any parent's duty, especially when the respect of an elderly person was at stake or the well-being of someone else was in jeopardy.

Children were considered special creatures. You would always hear someone saying, "Just for the children's sake." They were left to enjoy their childhood. At first sight it was very difficult to spot a rude child, since most of the time the child's bad behaviour would be absorbed by the group, the children keeping it among themselves. Children were left to play unsupervised amongst one another and do most of their naughty acts out of sight of any parent. A parent playing with his or her child was an alien practice. In short, it didn't exist. Any parent would just tell his or her child to go and play with their friends. They didn't tell them where to go because they knew that nothing would happen to them, even if they disappeared all day. They knew they would be in good hands or in someone's care where food was not an issue.

The majority of people, who came to welcome Dada and his guardian, lived in the quarter called Kabangu. The quarter was named after the river Kabangu, which is on the western side and goes on to meet the river Kwilu, which is on the northern side; this meets the river Kassai that in turn flows into the river Zaire that ends at the Atlantic Ocean. Kabangu is a river that flows fast compared to Kwilu. But Kwilu is twice the size of Kabangu. Kabangu looks dark, but when you collect its water in your hands, it's surprisingly clear, almost like the notorious river MayiNdombe (black water) en-route between Kenge and Kinshasa. Kabangu is not as dangerous as Mayi-Ndombe which has claimed many lives.

It's not a surprise to hear of an accident on the bridge of Mayi-Ndombe, which mysteriously sends cars into the river. Once a car or a lorry is drowning in Mayi-Ndombe, nothing gets found. They just disappear.

For the boy, the origin of the quarter's name was not important at that moment. What was troubling him was the fact that among the people who came to welcome him at 'Barriere' there were no girls of his age, just boys. He was asking himself if there were no young girls in this town.

The atmosphere at Barriere was very pleasant.

After a while Mr. Masa said to the crowd, "Good people, it is now time to go home. I think the boy is tired and in need of some rest."

Everybody agreed and made their way home.

Chapter 2

Bulungu was a small, but lively town. Even in early morning one noticed that the main high street was full of people, especially near the market. During the day people frequently made their way up and down the high street. One would hear people saying to one another: "Mbote na nge" (Hello), or "Ebwe?" (How are you?), which are common forms of salutation in a language called Kikongo. One could hear young people saying to some women, "Mama nge ikele mbote?" (Are you alright, mother?), and they mostly replied, "Munu kele mbote, mwana" (I am fine, my child). Although the Kikongo language was one of the national languages of Zaire besides Tshiluba, Lingala, Kishuahili and French, it had not always been the only language of conversation in Bulungu. It also has many versions.

Bulungu was considered the focal point of many nearby dialects such as Kimbala, Kihungana, Kiyanzi, Kisongo, etc. But most of the greetings were in Kikongo, as it was regarded as everybody's language. Kikongo is mainly spoken in the west of Zaire, where it can be traced back in history as far as the fifteenth century—to the Kingdom of Kongo, where the famous King Nzinga A Nkuvu, the fifteenth century Bakongo King who came into contact with the Portuguese and converted to Catholicism, took the name of Joao I.

Many people in Bulungu only distinguished two types of Kikongo: the Kikongo of 'Vova' (Speak) which is considered to be the oldest version, and the Kikongo of 'Munu kutuba' (I am speaking), the most modern version. The 'Munu kutuba' is for some reason the most preferred one in Bulungu, and it is also known as the 'Kikongo ya leta' (Kikongo of the state), especially by the Lingala-speaking people who live in Kinshasa, the capital of Zaire. There are many speculations about the origin of this version of Kikongo; but most people in Bulungu are convinced it was as a result of colonisation that it became established as a means of communication between the European masters and the native Kongolese. At the time of the Congo Free State in the late nineteenth century and during the construction of the railway from Matadi to Port Francky, the need of communication between the two parties was growing phenomenally. The construction project was a very serious and vital one. Many western European companies had an interest on it. They had heavily invested in the project that would contribute to the development of their companies and also their countries. At that particular time there was a need to transport the newly discovered raw materials out of the Dark Continent to Europe, thanks to Henry Motor Stanley, the British explorer and journalist. The authority at the time tried desperately and effectively to establish one language, which would improve communication with the workers who were mostly Kongolese or Bakongo people, for the route was very important for the Belgium economy. Thus the 'dit' version of Kikongo became close to Lingala, as the latter had already been established as the official language of the colonial army or public force.

The town of Bulungu is actually itself the capital of the zone of Bulungu. It is why during the day the town of Bulungu is always full with people, for it is heavily used as a centre for transaction or a trading place for the inhabitants of neighbouring villages. For most merchants, this is the place to be. For some *villagois* this is the closest you can get to urban life. For some expatriates, this is the place where tradition goes hand in hand with modern life. That harmony can best be appreciated by recognising the flow of the *'Chi'* in town. Any Chinese, who visited Bulungu, especially the quarter of Kabangu, always said that the first settlers of that place had a very strong knowledge of *Feng Shui* and applied it during the planning of the town.

The town of Bulungu also has a considerable population of Europeans, especially the Portuguese, and they are very useful to the local economy. Most of their business is food related. The people of Bulungu believe that the Portuguese love their town because of its geographic location. Although they are officially in the food business, some people say that they are also in the wood trade.

Bulungu is also a harbour town of one of Zaire's big river called Kwilu. The presence of this river has proven profitable to the Europeans' businesses. They don't have to depend only on the badly maintained roads that link the town to Kinshasa. It was common knowledge in Bulungu that the construction and the maintenance of roads were not on General Mobutu Sese-Seko's government priority list. Depending on the existing roads to transport goods, especially in a remote area, was a serious gamble with low returns, a gamble that no sensible businessman could take. So the Kwilu River offered another means of transportation. The river Kwilu also brought coolness, which might explain why the Europeans built their houses near its banks. In so many respects the river is a valuable business asset.

Kabangu River, although not used for the transportation of goods, is the most favoured one among young people. It is also the river that most parents allowed their children to go to have a bath and swim. It has been said that sometimes children were not permitted to go alone to the river because of the phenomena known in Bulungu as *ngandu ya munzenza*, which can literally be translated as the 'foreign crocodile' phenomena. It might be explained as the moment when there is a crocodile in the river with the mission of capturing children. The crocodiles, in this case, are actually human beings who have mastered the fourth dimension or have some sort of witch power that requires human blood; or they practice some kind of supernatural rituals that require human sacrifices. These human beings are said to be capable of transforming themselves from the human state to any reptile form. It was known in Bulungu that those who conduct such practices would have to drink human blood or eat human flesh during their rituals to keep up and vitalize their spiritual standards.

In time people became more knowledgeable as to where those shape-shifting humans lived, causing them to encounter more resistance in their home villages; so they opted to move close to foreign places or a river in the guise of any reptile, especially that of a crocodile, in order to capture their victims. Using this strategy, they believed, would avoid suspicion amongst local people and allow them to catch innocent children as they pleased. It was common knowledge in Bulungu that these people needed children's blood because they believed it to be pure. A death arising from these would not cause anyone to think of witches.

For the Bulungu inhabitants, only the deaths of elderly people were acceptable. When it came to the death of a young person, his or her uncle would have to explain and convince the whole population that the death was natural. Otherwise he would be accused of bewitching his own nephew or niece and may receive some physical abuse from the population. If such uncles did not want to be abused or accused of anything related to the death of their nephews or nieces, they were well advised to initiate what was known as supernatural investigation, which would lead to the real criminal or criminals. The investigation took many forms, the most common one being to visit the witch doctor to find out from the spirits who was responsible for the death. No one would even think of going to the witch doctor when it came to a situation where a child was killed or captured by a crocodile in the river. In this case everybody would blame the parent, especially the mother, for not training the poor child to recognise the presence of the crocodile in the river by being able to smell the crocodile once he or she was close to the river.

This phenomenon of children dying at the river Kabangu was a very serious matter and those 'crocodiles' had their good time. But suddenly everything changed when a strange man by the name of Papa Simon moved to Bulungu. He had the supernatural power or ability to know when those foreign crocodiles came to hunt. To everybody, Papa Simon looked like most middle-aged men with no strange physical characteristics that would cause suspicion. Though he lived with his newly wed wife, who was a local girl, his origin was a mystery. Possibly his wife knew something! According to him, he was asleep when his ancestors visited him in his dream to give him the power to stop the crocodiles' business in Bulungu. At that point, according to him, he left his village, which was also a mystery to the people of the Kabangu quarter. No one cared to know Papa Simon's real identity as long he was preventing the death of the poor children. He explained to people the true nature of those crocodiles. He told them that while he was in his village, he did not know or had heard of Bulungu; he was simply conducted and directed to the Kabangu area by the spirits of his ancestors, he said.

Before Papa Simon's arrival, the people of Bulungu were very naive regarding the crocodile phenomena. He single-handedly opened their eyes, for he was the one who told them that those deaths were not accidents.

That explained why the whole population looked up to him. They saw him as some kind of saviour. He also told them that for those phenomena to occur on such a scale and for such a long time, there had to be local accomplices. He even claimed that he could recognise them but, for some unknown reason, declined to give their names. Prior to Papa Simon's arrival Kabangu quarter was a very quiet place, especially after six o'clock in the evening. Since he came to the area, there was a visible change. Some evenings he could be seen going up and down every single road shouting like a hungry lion looking for food, saying something like, "Mothers and fathers who live in this street, listen to me carefully! From tomorrow do not let your children go to Kabangu River alone. There is right now a *ngandu ya munzenza* who is looking for children to capture. Do not take my words lightly! Contact the head of your street to know what to do!" He would keep on shouting while passing the street from one end to the other. He would repeat the warning as many times as he could until he had traversed all the roads in the Kabangu area.

He used to do this without a microphone, for his voice was very clear and loud and he did not need a *haut parleur.* Next day he would be the subject of conversations amongst the teenagers. One would say, "He must be a gifted man, he is guided by the spirits!"

"Come on," another would reply, "how can you prove that what he is saying is true?"

"Even if you do not believe him, at least you can appreciate his talent as a very good speaker."

Despite all the crocodile dramas, Kabangu area is a lovely place to live. It is a middleclass neighbourhood. In that area most women are housewives. You'll always find someone around, especially mothers preparing the meal for their husbands and children. Most children in the area attended the Catholic Primary School, which had very strict rules. The pupils studied to a high standard. Disciplining a pupil was the norm.

There were only three Catholic primary schools, two for boys and one for girls. The policy of the local Catholic authority was that girls and boys should be educated and kept apart. There were no excuses for a boy and girl relationship.

Chapter 3

It took them a while to get to Mr. Masa's house even when they took a short cut. They had to stop at every single house on their way to chat with people. That was common practice in the neighbourhood. This way of life did not annoy Dada. He was amused and enjoyed the show. But he didn't like those prayers to the ancestors for his protection. He thought of it as primitive. He hadn't yet arrived at the understanding of this kind of spiritual world. He was concerned that he might have nightmares after listening to those prayers. That was why he didn't want to focus too much on them. He didn't want to start thinking of death and ghosts.

When they arrived at home they were with friends who where very close to Mr. Masa. On their arrival Sylvan, the houseboy, greeted them and took the luggage from those who had helped Mr. Masa carry it to the house. He did this every time his boss returned from a journey. After arranging the bathing facilities for Dada, Sylvan told his boss, "Everything is done," avoiding eye contact with him.

"What about the boy?" Mr. Masa asked. "Did you fix everything?"

"Yes, the water is in the bathroom."

"Did you put in the warm water?"

"Yes sir, and I have also used the new red plastic container that you brought from Kikwiti last month," responded the houseboy.

At that particular time, Dada was sitting on the long chair under the shade at the front of the house, enjoying the sun. His guardian came towards him and said, "It is time for you to bath now. I know that you are very tired, but after this long journey you can only feel better after taking a warm bath."

"Yes sir," said Dada.

"Go with Sylvan," said his guardian. "He'll show you everything."

Dada went into his room to fetch a towel, the one bought by his mother in Kinshasa before he left. Sylvan was waiting for him and when Dada was ready he told him, "I know you'll be surprised because the bathroom is not inside the house, but outside."

Dada remained quiet, walking next to Sylvan as they went out of the house.

"Can you see that little bungalow at the corner of the compound behind the house?" Sylvan asked.

"Yes," replied Dada.

"That's where you'll be washing yourself."

Sylvan took him inside and showed him all he needed to know. The condition of the place he would be taking a bath in was unbearable for him, but he had no other option. After thinking about people who had bathed there and were still in good health, Dada thought of what his mother used to tell him about her own childhood. He recalled everything she said, especially about how poor they were when she was a child but managed to be happy. Then he realised how much he missed his family. Before he even started to bath the tears began to well out of his eyes.

After his bath Dada went outside and everything once more seemed normal.

Because Mr. Masa was a single man, Dada was to be taken care of by Sylvan the houseboy. His guardian gave him a lecture about the house and the area they lived in. He was taught how to conform to his new society. The talk took longer than Dada expected. He did not ask any questions about special circumstances.

After the sun set, Mr. Masa called Dada and said to him, "I believe you must be very tired—it is time for you to go to sleep. Tomorrow I may have to take you to school. I'm sure you will like it. It's a very good school and everyone is very nice."

"Yes, euh! Buh! Can I ask a question?"

"Yes, of course", said Mr. Masa, "but take a seat first. I want you to tell me anything you like; and remember, from now on I am your father, so don't be afraid to ask me any question on anything."

Mr. Masa took the boy to his room where his luggage was still unpacked and sat on the edge of the bed. He told Dada to take the chair, which was next to the reading desk and sit on it. To make Dada even more comfortable, he looked at him, smiling, and told him to speak freely. After a short time Dada, without looking at his guardian since it was not polite to look a superior in the eyes when talking to him, said, almost in tears, "When will I go back to Kinshasa?"

"Let me ask you something. Do you know why you are here?"

"Yes, sir," replied Dada.

"No, I don't think so," his guardian said, smiling kindly. "Let me explain. Your family has just gone abroad to the U.S.A. for a diplomatic mission. This means your father is going to be the Zairian Ambassador at the United Nations. He is going to be based in New York. You know that being the first son in a family like yours, you have to be educated in a certain way—so that one day, in the near future even, you will lead your family and probably hold an important post in the central government at Kinshasa. This being the situation, you must be able to accept life in a certain way. Your two big sisters and younger brother will be proud of you when they return from the U.S.A."

"Yes," Dada answered, still not looking his new father in the eyes.

"And your father," continued Mr. Masa, "wants to make you the man of tomorrow. He cares about you. He would like you to get what he calls real education. He thinks that the countryside is the appropriate place for you to get that kind of education, and maybe the experience will open your eyes to a lot of things that can also make you a strong man. One day in the future, when you will have to lead our people, you will know how to relate to everyone. I am telling you 'easy come, easy go.' Your father and mother worked hard to be who they are today. They want you to understand our culture and be prepared for the future. You represent their future. Get yourself ready to be part of this society. I know you are only ten years old and I understand how you feel, but you have no choice."

When he had finished, Mr. Masa put his left hand on Dada head to give him some kind of comfort. He stood up and went to his room after wishing Dada a good sleep and telling him that if he needed something he should come and ask with no fear since Sylvan did not stay overnight.

After a short time Mr. Masa revisited Dada's room to see if he was comfortable and coping with his new situation. Then he closed the door and went to his bedroom. The house had no electricity, which Dada had a serious problem coming to terms with, especially since he could not say anything. Before he went to sleep he comforted himself with the thought that these conditions were necessary for him to be a man.

Chapter 4

Mr. Masa was the first to get up. He went to Dada's room and knocked at the door. "It's time to get up, Dada," he announced. "We have a lot to do today." Then he went back to his room.

Dada got up and went first to his guardian's room for the morning blessing and anything special he would have to know before he went to take a bath.

Sylvan did not come to work very early so Mr. Masa handled all the housework himself.

Dada got himself ready, took a bath and dressed as required by his new father. Mr. Masa made the breakfast and called Dada to the table. As a member of the Lutheran Protestant Church he didn't have to memorise a prayer. He was also aware of Dada's Roman Catholic background and his lack of understanding of his way of praying. To avoid any misunderstanding, he asked Dada if he knew how Protestants pray.

"Yes," Dada answered with his eyes on the meal.

"How do you pray before you eat?" asked Mr. Masa.

"Maman taught us a prayer in Tshiluba which we had to memorise."

"Is that prayer in Catechise?" asked Mr. Masa.

"No," said Dada.

"Okay," Mr. Masa nodded. "I now see that you will not be surprised by my way of praying."

There was silence in the dining room. Nobody said anything. Dada wanted to say something but felt that this was not the appropriate moment to talk. He also knew that well raised children should always ask for permission before talking to older people. They were taught not to interrupt someone while they were in the middle of a sentence, and to talk less about themselves to other people—unless it was for a special reason.

The silence was interrupted when Mr. Masa looked at Dada and said, "Close your eyes and let us pray." Mr. Masa closed his eyes and said, "Thank you, Almighty God, for keeping us alive after the long journey from Kinshasa, and also for protecting us from any evil attack. Thank you for this breakfast, and we ask for your protection and blessing throughout the day. In the name of Jesus Christ, Amen."

Dada was very surprised that there was no rosary, no picture of a Saint, not even a mention of Saint Mary. "Well, this was not the time for trying to know too much," he said to himself. After having breakfast in peace Mr. Masa started lecturing Dada again about the society in which he would be living. He was focusing on the boy's behaviour in his new school. Dada listened attentively.

Mr. Masa continued: "Be polite to everybody you come in contact with. Respect everyone's parents and consider them as your own. If you have any problem, let me know. A lot of children will try to bully you but don't fight them, tell your teacher. Speak less about yourself. Lots of people here are *feticheurs*."

He went on to explain what they were going to do during the day and Dada prepared himself for school. He was thinking about his family while getting ready.

Apart from Mr. Masa's presence, he hated everything around him. No electricity. No car to take him to school. No bodyguard to protect him in case of violence. Maybe things would change in the near future, he kept telling himself. He didn't like the way his parents chose to educate him. If they didn't want to spoil him, he kept on saying to himself, why did they expose him to the luxuries of life only to put him in these appalling conditions? "You can live in the U.S.A.," he thought to himself, "and still know how to relate to your own people." He pictured Mohammed-Ali who was born and raised in the U.S.A. but still considered himself African.

For the moment he had to deal with the reality of Bulungu. Whatever happened he would not see his family for at least two years—not until he got his national certificate to testify to the completion of primary school.

After putting all the dirty plates in the kitchen for Sylvan to take care of when he came, Mr. Masa told Dada it was time to go to school for his enrolment.

Chapter 5

Mr. Masa believed that Dada needed to know the short cut to school, even though it was complicated. Using the high road to go to school was not Mr. Masa's preferred choice, although it would be easier for Dada to remember. He preferred the short cut, mainly because one didn't have to go through the market to reach the school; also, at this time of the morning, people were setting up their goods.

In Bulungu the market was not only where people traded, but a place where they got the latest gossip and where most rumours began. Passing through the market when one was in a hurry was not the best choice. One always bumped into someone one knew and one would end up spending half an hour or more talking without realising it. So for Mr. Masa this was not an option.

They left the house by the front gate of the compound. It was at that very moment that Dada started to appreciate the beauty of their neighbourhood. All the houses, at least as far as he could see, looked alike. The lines of beautiful and colourful flowers separated the compounds of all the houses. The palm trees lined the roadsides. It seemed like everyone in the area was an expert in geometry and botany. The rose was the most common flower.

Once outside the gate, they turned right to go to Dada's new school. This was unusual for Mr. Masa because he always turned left to go to his workplace. While they were still in Gobary Road, where they lived, Dada asked if he could pick one of the flowers to play with. "Ha! Ha!" laughed his guardian, "it's easy for someone to notice that you're not from here. Do not embarrass yourself in school by saying such things in front of the other pupils. This is one of the ways we recognise newcomers!" For whatever reason, they stayed quiet when crossing the football field and also the small plantation that belonged to the local Catholic Church. It took them less than half an hour to reach Dada's new school.

On arrival they went straight to the main office instead of satisfying Dada's desire to explore the area before doing anything else. The natural beauty of the school absorbed him. The buildings were not as attractive as his previous school, but the school had a very big square compound. There were two schools in the compound. They were Mawete and Ngemba, situated respectively at the south and north extremities of the compound, the two buildings facing each other. At the extreme west of the compound was the main office that housed the headmaster's office and all the administrative and finance offices. At the extreme east was the Church. This magnificent building reflected the seriousness of the local Catholic hierarchy regarding Godly matters. The architecture of the Church generated energy of goodwill, which could be felt by anyone on the right wavelength. At first sight one would know this was the job of a top mathematician who had the knowledge of applied aesthetics and who was also a true Catholic believer.

Once inside the main office, a short man who was clearly happy to see Mr. Masa led them to the headmaster's office. Mr. Masa did not need formalities or an appointment to see the headmaster. Both headmasters shared the building, but Mr. Mongeme of Mawete primary school was Mr. Masa's good friend. After greeting a few people, Mr. Masa knocked at Mr. Mongeme's door.

"Who is that?" said the headmaster.

"It's me," replied Mr. Masa.

The headmaster happily opened the door, greeted them and invited them inside his office. Once inside he offered them a seat. He was not surprised to see them in his office as he was among the few close friends of Mr. Masa who knew about Dada coming to Bulungu. He had seen Dada's photo before. Dada didn't need formal enrolment and everything was done before his arrival in the town anyway. After a brief chat, Mr. Mongeme explained to his friend that he would like the boy to be in the class of Ms Betika. According to the headmaster Dada needed to be in a class where the teacher was a woman.

"This will help him," said the headmaster. "Having a woman figure head around, he will still hold his high moral values; and to a certain extent she might also replace his mother."

"That is not a problem," replied Mr. Masa.

"You're not married yet," said Mr. Mongeme, "and since you're a very busy person, I thought the boy would need to be close to someone else. That is why I thought Ms Betika's class would be appropriate for him. I told her everything two weeks ago."

"Do whatever you think is best for all of us," said Mr. Masa to his friend.

They carried on discussing what they thought was good for Dada, who was quiet as they expected him to be. They did not even ask him for his opinion. At that moment he was almost absent physically as the two were in deep and serious conversation regarding his future. They acted as if he wasn't even there. Mr. Mongeme asked his friend about their journey and also why he didn't wait for at least two weeks before bringing Dada to school. As an experienced primary school headmaster, Mr. Mongeme believed the boy should have relaxed and got himself familiar with his new hometown before coming to school.

Mr. Masa started again to tell his friend the story from point zero. He explained how he was told about the boy. "I believe this opportunity will make my connection to the boy's family even stronger," he said. Then he talked about their journey again, emphasising that nothing special or unusual happened. Dada was still quiet while the two men talked to each other.

"When we arrived at Pascal in Kinshasa," continued Mr. Masa, "the place was very empty. It was also very hot."

"And then what did you do?" enquired the headmaster.

"I don't know why the place was empty," replied Mr. Masa. "We had to wait for the lorry to come so we went and sat in a bar. It was the bar you and I always choose to relax in when we're waiting for our transport. There's a new one close to it. It is called…um…um…let me think again,…um…Oh, it's not that important."

"Which one are you talking about?" asked the headmaster.

"El Dorado, *now* I remember, El Dorado," said Mr. Masa to his friend. "I know that you know it."

"I don't see why you had to take the young boy to such a place, even if it was very hot."

"Well, I did," replied Mr. Masa.

"I don't want to take up your time," said the headmaster. "I will come to your house tonight and then we can talk properly. Let me call up the secretary to take the boy around and he can meet his teacher and new classmates."

He called the secretary to take Dada to visit his new school. Ms Betika was the only woman teacher in Mawete primary school. She was known for her strict rules. She was in her late thirties but her exact age was a mystery to her pupils. No one apparently cared. There were a lot of rumours about her. Some said she was from an upper class and very rich family and that was why she just enjoyed teaching and nothing else. It was common knowledge that money didn't affect her commitment to teaching. Providing knowledge and moral values to all of her pupils, underprivileged kids or not, that was what she was known for. Even in times of poor funding for the school by the department of education, she was still committed to providing a high standard of teaching. Most of her pupils always said she cared about them as if they were her own children. In most cases one could recognise her pupils in the middle of a crowd as they always stood out. They were very respectful. They were always very clean and they always carried a book, unless they were taking part in some sort of outdoor activity. She always managed somehow to visit all her pupils at their home. She made sure she knew their parents personally. This was probably why the headmaster thought she would be the best person to be Dada's teacher. Perhaps it was because his guardian was single and a very busy person that Mr. Mongeme concluded Ms Betika would be the best choice. Or maybe it was because the headmaster thought Dada needed a mother figure. Ms Betika was a woman of mystery. No one seemed to know exactly what she was after. She had a very distinctive face and wore glasses that could not be bought in town and consequently had to be prescribed. She was approximately one metre seventy centimetres tall, and slim. These features didn't make her a beautiful woman in terms of local culture that dictated that a beautiful woman had to be big. One always heard men saying, "How can somebody marry a woman with no flesh on her bones!" Slim women always had a hard time when it came to finding a husband—unless it was an arranged marriage.

That was not the path Ms Betika wanted to take. It was why most slim women preferred to concentrate on studying or business. Ms Betika did not show any signs of desperation of any sort and that was why people did not care much about her feelings. Some people who knew her well, outside school, always said she was a very soft and understanding woman; but they could not convince her pupils who knew her as a very hard and tough teacher.

Some pupils in Mawete primary school said that it took them about five years before they saw Ms Betika laugh in public. She was a very respected teacher around the town. All her pupils, past and present, loved her very much and were proud of her, even though she was strict with them. Despite her family wealth and possessions, she preferred to live in Manzanza neighbourhood instead of the area where all the European people lived.

The Zairians who chose to live in the same place with the Europeans were the very successful businessmen or the officials who represented the Central Government of Kinshasa, and also officials of the state party, called *Mouvement Populaire de la Revolution*—MPR in short.

Chapter 6

After one long week of boring life in his new neighbourhood, Dada still didn't know how he could make Bulungu a better place to live in. For some reason he was not told about, he had to stay one week at home before he started school. At first he thought it was a good idea as he would have the opportunity to familiarise himself with his new life, but staying alone at home all day wasn't pleasant at all.

He asked himself, how could he become familiar with his new environment if he did not have the chance to explore it properly. At that particular moment his answer hardly mattered. To survive in this town he would have to spend more time dreaming than complaining. He believed that daydreaming could help him fight loneliness, which was becoming his way of life in Bulungu. While he was enjoying one of his favourite dreams, sitting alone under the tree at the front of the house on a very hot and sunny day, Sylvan came to him and said, "What would you like to eat this evening?"

"Anything that is available," Dada replied.

"You seem to be unhappy today."

"No, I am fine." Dada pretended to be relaxed when he was with Sylvan.

It was only a short time afterwards that Mr. Masa showed up at home. As usual he went to Dada to find out what he had done during the day.

The usual question was, "Did you eat?" And Dada always answered, "Yes Sir."

There was not much that Mr. Masa could ask the boy, for he had not yet started school. He thought he could not offer much at this stage except food and some material needs, which were readily available at home. There was nothing else that Dada needed. He had clothes and there was plenty of food in the house. He hadn't started school, so there was nothing he needed. When Mr. Masa arrived, even late, he always brought a feeling of security to Dada. And, indeed, Dada was always happy to know that his guardian was there.

Because of his repeated absence from home, Mr. Masa might have seemed like a stranger to Dada, but that was not his main concern. He always tried to remind the boy of the sole purpose of his presence in the town. He kept telling him that to be a great person in the future one had to make sacrifices at some point in one's life. "One does not build a house in one day," he said.

After being in his room, Mr. Masa came out in his casual clothes and asked Sylvan to bring him a chair to sit under the tree where Dada was resting. At that time, sunset, everyone was expected to be at home with his or her family.

Everything was done as he requested and he went to sit near Dada. It was a very good evening. A big and clear reddish sun was setting at the other side of the town. The fresh air was accessible to every body. The peace was not even disturbed by Papa Simon who gave no warning about the foreign crocodiles. For some reason, the flowers in the compound looked more beautiful than ever. There were not many people in the street. There were small lights outside every house that Dada could see from where he was sitting. Most mothers had just arrived from the forest where they went to take care of their plantation and fish pounds. It was as though they were all connected in some sort of harmonisation or co-ordination in their activities.

In Dada's eyes, everything looked like a film set or a theatrical backdrop, like a *mise en scene*. The harmony, the babies crying on one side, the adults laughing on the other side, amazed him. In his imagination he conceived a picture of how people in all the houses were very happy, except him. All the houses had a complete family structure. Fathers and mothers were taking care of their children. He believed he was the only one who was not perfectly happy in this idyllic neighbourhood.

Sitting beside him, Mr. Masa asked Dada to call Sylvan. Dada did so, and when the houseboy arrived, Mr. Masa started his usual lecture—though today he sounded a little different. "Today," he explained, "I have just received a very important message about my new role in the Bulungu teachers association. I have been chosen to go back to Kinshasa to discuss the matter regarding teachers' wages. I don't know how long it will take or how long I will be away. Sylvan, you will start living here and take care of Dada. My secretary will be coming here sometimes to provide any necessary help."

When he stopped talking there was complete silence. He was not surprised as he expected it from them.

"Sylvan," he continued, "you'll take care of Dada and then show him the way to school so he will learn to do everything by himself." After pausing for a short while he looked at Sylvan who was standing next to them, at the same time placing his hand on Dada's arm. "This boy is my future," he said. "Take care of him and show him how he can be independent. Take him to the river and show him how to swim. You should discipline him if you think he is misbehaving. I'm sure you both understand me very well."

They both answered yes. They thought he had finished but he carried on again.

"I almost forgot. I'm leaving tomorrow for Kikwiti; from there I will get the transport to Kinshasa."

Dada didn't know what to feel, happy or sad. But he was well aware that his opinions didn't count.

CHAPTER 7

After Mr. Masa's departure, Sylvan took the responsibility of taking care of Dada. He showed him how to get around in Bulungu. He took him to school, then to his classroom. The first day Dada came into the classroom the teacher welcomed him. It was a rule of the school to make newcomers feel privileged among other pupils. Once inside the classroom, Ms Betika asked the new pupil to introduce himself, and Dada did as requested by the teacher.

On his first day in the classroom, Dada made a very good impression on the other pupils and the teacher. He struck everyone as being a most polite and well-raised boy. He was well dressed for an average Bulungu pupil. There were no doubts about his family background. He wore a very clean white shirt and blue shorts, which looked expensive. His appearance might have given the impression that he was not one of the other pupils, for while everybody else wore blue shirts and shorts as the school uniform, he was wearing white and blue. He was, in fact, given the exceptional privilege of wearing a different school uniform. On his feet he had a pair of smart new black shoes. One would have to be from Kinshasa to know that this was a top range shoe called Campus, which cost a fortune. But even without knowing the label, one could see how expensive they looked. With his clean pair of white socks and expensive shoes Dada's background was unmistakable, and it was easy to see he was a newcomer to town. While it was common for the pupils in Bulungu to wear a pair of sandals, a proper pair of leather shoes was normally what the teachers wore.

Dada had nice clean outfits, which perplexed many of the pupils. The rules of Ms Betika's classroom were that a pupil should stand in front of the class, if chosen, to tell a story. For Dada this was not his lucky day. He was chosen by the teacher to tell a story about himself and had been told to go to the front of the classroom. He was not pleased because he hated being in front of people. He had no choice, however. He went to the front of the class and introduced himself as Dada Tshienda from Easter Kassai Province, though he was, he explained, born in Kinshasa!

He said, "My father is the new Zairean Ambassador in the United Nations."

Except for the teacher, no one else could believe or understand that his father's job of Ambassador made him a very important person. In the eyes of his new classmates, his father may even be a friend of the President Mobutu. It would take a lot of effort to convince those boys that they might be sitting next to someone who knew the President personally.

After Dada finished his talk the teacher told the rest of the class, "You all need to help him enjoy this class." They all agreed. Dada, in fact, was pleased with his first day in Ms Betika's class. The pupils were very polite to the teacher and to each other. On that first day at school during the break, Dada had already made friends. Almost everyone wanted to talk to him. Once again he was in the spotlight.

Sylvan didn't have to go and fetch Dada from school at twelve o'clock, as the teacher told him that Dada should not be treated as a baby. No parent goes to collect his or her child from school. The children go to school and come home by themselves, or in a group of friends. Michael, one of his classmates, asked Dada if he would like to walk home with the group since they all lived in the same street. Dada said he would and walked home with them. Even though they looked friendly, he sensed that his new friends were not comfortable with the news of his family background.

"Is it true?" asked one of his new friends while they were walking home. "Is it really true that you come from Kinshasa?"

"Yes," Dada answered.

"Are you sure?"

"Yes."

"Don't think we are stupid! If you want to be one of us, you must tell us the truth every time."

Dada was scared but remained calm as though he were in control of the situation. They continued walking home and passed through the church garden talking about something else. It was only when they reached the football field that the same boy who asked Dada questions started again.

"You think that if you tell everyone that you come from the capital you will get special treatment? Let me warn you now so that everybody can hear. If any of my sisters asks me about you, you will be in real trouble and you'll not be one of us anymore!"

A complete silence followed before the boy carried on, once again intimidating poor Dada.

For Dada the morning had not been bad, but now everything seemed to be turning upside down. He kept on telling himself that everything would be all right. When they arrived near the other end of the football field, Bony, one of the boys who was with them, said, "I don't like someone who lies!" At this point Dada had no clue how to respond. Then Bony stood in front of Dada and ordered him to stop. When Dada tried to move forward, Bony pushed him back. Dada stopped and wondered why his new friends were not stopping Bony from harassing him. Not all of them stopped immediately to see what was going on.

"Where did you get your uniform from?" Bony asked Dada.

"My…my mother gave it to me."

"Where is your mother?"

"My mother and all my family are now in the United States of America for…"

Dada hadn't even finished his sentence when the sound of the slap on his face made all the boys freeze. No one could believe what Bony had just done. They all moved closer to see what was happening.

Dada was lying on the ground and Bony was holding a stick in his hand. Everything happened so fast that no-one could count how many times Dada was punched or how many times Bony used the stick to beat him. Dada had his face to the ground when one of them tried to help him get up. When the others looked at him they saw that his face and uniform were covered with blood. They could not see any cut on his face, but they could see blood coming from his little nose. No one among his new friends visibly expressed any concern at Dada's situation. The only thing one of them said was, "This is our way of life."

Dada didn't cry. He just kept quiet. It didn't take much to realise that this was some sort of conspiracy generated by jealousy. No one came to his rescue; they all stood there as if no one was in pain.

They all left and Dada was alone, bleeding under the sun.

CHAPTER 8

▼

Sylvan was alone in the house, cleaning and putting everything in place. The food was already prepared. He was just waiting for Dada to come home to get his VIP treatment before he went back to school at 2 p.m. for the afternoon session.

While he was in the dining room fixing the table, he heard people screaming outside the front door. He quickly realised they were young girls but he could not understand what they were saying. He almost collapsed when he went out of the house and saw Dada, in front of a small group of small girls, bleeding. He lost control of himself. He went inside the house and rushed back. With both hands on top of his head, Sylvan didn't know what to do or where to start! He finally stood in front of Dada with his mouth wide open but saying nothing. At that instant Dada could see Sylvan experiencing his end of the world. Sylvan did not know what to say and knew for sure he would be blamed for the incident. He also believed there was no way Mr. Masa would keep him on. For Sylvan, losing his job was also losing his status. Within a short time there were a lot of people in the compound. Sylvan recovered quickly and took the boy inside the house. Once inside, he did everything to make Dada comfortable. After a short while people dispersed and Dada was left with Sylvan.

Dada did not have to go back to school that afternoon. Instead, he spent the afternoon under a tree in the back yard. Due to his traumatic experience he began to have mixed feelings about Bulungu.

The next day Dada's story was public knowledge.

At school everyone who was involved in Dada' misery was disciplined accordingly. This was something Bony and his friends hadn't expected. Since that day Sylvan started to take Dada to school himself. This gave Dada some confidence and he knew that he should not be afraid anymore. He adopted a positive attitude and thought of what his mother had told him about this kind of eventuality, and said to himself: "I don't think Bony would have done this to me if I was a useless person. This must be an initiation process or a special welcome from Bulungu's boys. I think I've got the message and I believe this incident has woken me up to the world of reality. I'll have to do everything to enjoy this town and I will not allow anyone else to make me feel sad. I have a mother who loves me—that's all I need!"

Just a few days had passed since the incident but it seemed like months to Dada since no-one bothered to talk about it. Dada was asleep when Mr. Masa returned from his trip. Sylvan did not wake him up. It was only in the morning that he was surprised to be told by Sylvan that Mr. Masa had come back last night and had already gone to work.

At this revelation Dada thought to himself that even his parents, who were very busy people, always brought him presents after a trip and met with him before they went to meet the President. He was important in their life.

He asked Sylvan if his guardian had asked about him when he came home yesterday.

He wasn't really surprised to find out that all Mr. Masa was interested in was his material well-being—whether there was enough food at home, and whether he was feeling well. He knew that Mr. Masa would never ask Sylvan if he was going to school, because he had to go, or if he was behaving in school, because there were strict rules in school and no-one was permitted to be an exception, or if he liked being in Bulungu.

As usual, he was taken to school by Sylvan but no longer liked it. He now wanted to be part of the society and to do what all the boys in the town were doing. At school, before the bell rang for all the pupils to stand in straight lines in front of the classrooms they were in, Dada went to look for Bony. Today was not Monday, which meant there would be no dancing and singing for President Mobutu and his state party called MPR, so Dada had all the time on his hands before class started.

It did not take him long to spot Bony, who was sitting on top of a dead tree that lay on the grass. He rushed to where Bony was sitting, but Bony didn't notice him since he was facing the grass. Dada greeted him by saying, "Bonjour!"

Dada could not fail to notice how Bony panicked when he heard his voice! When Bony raised his face to look at him, Dada could see the powerlessness in Bony.

Bony asked himself if this was the same person he had a problem with, or his double.

"What happened to you?" Dada asked him. "How come you are sitting alone at this place?"

"All of this is *your* fault," replied Bony.

"What do you mean?"

"Don't tell me that you don't know what's happening! I have a problem with everybody because of you! Even my own father beat me up because of you. No-one wants to talk to me anymore. I don't know…"

"You don't need to explain everything to me," Dada said. "I think we have a lot in common. We should meet at the end of the morning session. I have a plan. If everybody sees you and I together, maybe they will change their minds."

Just after their conversation the bell rung and it was time for each of them to go to his respective class.

Once inside the classroom Dada was already thinking of people's reaction when they saw him with Bony and saw how they had become good friends. Dada looked at everybody inside the classroom and realised that even though Ms Betika had not yet arrived, the pupils didn't talk to each other. There was absolute silence. Dada was becoming uncomfortable with these rules and regulations. After a short time Ms Betika entered the classroom.

As part of the regulations pupils had to stand up and greet her by saying: "Bonjour citoyenne Betika." She would reply, "Bonjour et asseyez vous." They would all sit down and the teaching would begin.

Today she made them sit down by means of a gesture of the hand and without greeting them. The only thing she said was for Dada to come outside with her. Poor Dada was wondering what he had done wrong for him to be disciplined.

Once outside Dada saw Mr. Masa standing there with another man that he had never seen before. There were four of them in total. Then Mr. Masa started talking to Ms Betika about Dada. Although Dada was present no-one took the time to ask him what he thought. Instead, they simply talked amongst themselves.

Dada was standing there quietly waiting for his turn to talk. Because he was not allowed to look at their faces when they were talking, he listened looking down. Mr. Masa was saying, "I'm leaving this afternoon and the boy could spend some time with you, especially at the weekend. In case of any problem Sylvan will contact you, and you can send me a telegram in Kinshasa."

"Okay, Dada," said Ms Betika. "You heard what your father had to say, so you can go inside to the classroom."

As he was about to leave, Mr. Masa addressed him directly, saying, "All your Sunday clothes are in my bedroom. You will need to wear them when you go to Church. Be nice and polite to everybody and I will see you when I get back."

It had been a long time since his guardian had said anything to him directly. Dada thought to himself, "Be back? Be back…be back from where? You don't even tell me where you are going, and now you're telling me you will be back. Back from where!" He continued thinking to himself, "What is the point of me being with them? If they want to make a decision they should just do it, then call me." Then he walked off to the classroom.

During break time he went to look for Bony as they were not in the some class, but he could not see him. He had learnt from another classmate of his that Bony had been banned from taking part in any recreation activity for some time. He felt so bad about Bony. How could he be left inside the class when everybody else was outside?

He decided to speak to Ms Betika about it if the opportunity arose, or if she allowed him to ask her any questions regarding his personal matters. As he turned to go back to his classroom at the end of the break, Ms Betika appeared behind him and said, "You do not seem to be happy, my son."

"Am I allowed to speak, miss?" replied Dada.

"Yes, of course."

"I am okay…"

"I understand," interrupted Ms Betika. "You don't need to feel left out. You are coming with me to my house today so you can find out more about this place." She looked at her watch and said, "It's almost the end of the break and time for you to go back inside." She pointed in the direction of the classroom.

So Dada left, thinking to himself, "Another one. What is wrong with this town, nobody seems to listen! At least my mother used to ask me how I felt about certain things."

During teaching time in the classroom everything appeared normal to Dada. At the end of the morning session he was not surprised when Ms Betika asked him to come with her for lunch at her house. After the class, he had to wait for his teacher to be ready for them to leave together to go to her house. He did not know if he had to be happy or sad about this invitation when he was planning to meet Bony to have a serious discussion about his plan of how to enjoy Bulungu.

He recalled some conversations with his mother. He remembered what his mother had told him about his father's work and he said to himself, "From now on I am going to be like my father. I cannot have a fight with someone if I am not sure that I will win it. I should be friends with everyone in Bulungu, especially in Kabangu."

After a short time Ms Betika was ready to go home for lunch, so they left. They took the small footpath, which was behind the headmaster's office, and went through the school garden where all the pupils had planted something, which they had to take care of every Wednesday afternoon as part of the school policy.

After just a few seconds, Dada found himself amongst a group of young girls. A lot of young girls, who lived in the Manzanza neighbourhood, preferred walking home with Ms Betika. Dada thought this was not a bad idea at all.

Ms Betika was very quiet. No one spoke until they reached their homes. Ms Betika said to each of them, every time they arrived at one of the girls' houses, "This is your house, see you soon."

Chapter 9

On arrival at Ms Betika's house, which took them approximately ten minutes to reach by foot, Dada quickly realised that Ms Betika was a well-organised person. Her house was well built and maintained. He could spot three servants who were there to keep Ms Betika comfortable. When they got inside the house they went straight to the dining table.

While inside the house, Dada could not see any evidence of another person living with her. Once at the table, he was surprised that Ms Betika did not say a prayer before they started eating. She just said to him, "Bon appetit," and he answered, "Merci." They had their meal in complete silence. As usual, he could not ask any questions. He had mixed feelings about the invitation. He thought to himself, "Should I regard Ms Betika as my guardian because Mr. Masa is never present? I will not think of Mr. Masa—he is never there for me anyway; so his absence doesn't make any difference."

After the meal Ms Betika told Dada to follow one of the servants who would show him where to relax outside the house. Dada was taken outside to sit under the tree as instructed by his teacher. He quickly enjoyed the idea of relaxing at his teacher's compound because there were no fences and he could see people around as well as their neighbours. He thought to himself, "All those people passing by, they have no idea of who I am! They don't even know that one day I could become the President of this country…Ah, that's life. I do not understand what is happening but this town is opening my eyes!" After a short time Dada saw his teacher coming out of the house to join him where he was sitting. She did not say anything but one of the servants knew that he had to bring her a relaxing chair for her to sit on before she went back to school for the afternoon session. After sitting comfortably she said to Dada, "I think now is a good time for us to talk," and she continued: "There are a lot of things you need to know about this town to make your life more interesting. This small town can be very nice to you, especially if you follow the rules. You will not find the rules written anywhere, you will pick them up. No-one will tell you about them. At first sight you see people very happy and united, but in reality this is not what is actually happening. You need to know that there is a sharp division between the young people, and some have this division from their parents. The kids here don't just play with everyone. There is a division between the Catholic and the Protestant children. Most of these people have no clue about their faith or doctrine but they are serious when it comes to defending it. Some young boys always look for a fight at any opportunity, but you need to be from here to link those fights to the division between the Churches. It seems no one is willing to resolve the problem; both churches play down the scale of the problem. Most of these boys belong to those Churches just because they were admitted to their schools. The problem is very complicated, and to fully understand it I would need all day to explain it to you. It's a social disaster. The representatives of the Central Government make the matter worse because they only send their children to this Catholic school. This means our school is well funded and we can provide a better standard of education. The Protestant children blame the Catholics for looking down on them because their church and schools are not well built compared to the Catholic buildings. Also they laugh at Catholics because they only have Europeans as priests. They also say people go to the Catholic Church just because of the buildings, not the teaching. The only thing that unites people in this town is the same thing that both the churches condemn. It is a tradition that they both call fetishism. It is preached in both churches that anyone who practices it will not get eternal life. Most of the parents in this place still practice it, but there is going to be serious problems for the next generation. Those who are born here are under constant pressure without realising it."

She paused for a second, then carried on. "Now let me talk to you about food. Every time you are invited to eat at someone's house, you don't need to thank the person who invited you for the meal, especially if that person is a close friend to you. I know that in Kinshasa food may be very important for most of the people but it's the contrary over here. They find it normal if one turns up at someone's house for a meal without being invited. I'm sure you will notice that people here send cooked meals to each other in the evenings. This is the tradition people have developed over the years. One thing you should not do is to stay at someone's home, not even your best friends, when it is raining, and when…"

"Excuse me, madam!" interrupted one of the servants. "There is a snake in the chicken house right now. What should I do?"

"What! A snake! In the chicken house? Call Paul right now!" screamed Ms Betika.

At that time Dada did not know what to say. A snake near where he was sitting—he could not believe it! He was scared to death but didn't want to admit to it or to show it to his teacher. "What kind of place is this town!" he thought to himself. "A snake can easily come close to where people live! I wish my sisters were here to witness this because they would never believe me if I told them."

In a few seconds Paul, the servant who had been with Ms Betika for a very long time, came and stood in front of them and said, "Yes madam?"

"Paul, what is happening with you?" asked Ms Betika.

"I am fine, madam."

"Okay, you," she said, talking to the servant who found the snake. "You can go and do the washing up. I don't want you to take any risk of killing a snake; you're still a young man. Paul has more experience in handling snakes, so you don't needn't worry—everything is going to be fine."

It was only then that Paul realised what was going on. In the meantime, poor Dada couldn't understand what was happening! He thought it was strange because there was a snake not far from were they were sitting, yet people were taking their time and were quite relaxed about it!

He thought to himself, "This would be a serious matter if it was at my house in Kinshasa! We would even be moved so that all the house could be checked properly, and that could take days; but here Ms Betika is taking her time!"

Then he heard his teacher asking Paul when the other servant left, "Do you know what time this is?"

"I'm sorry," the servant replied. "I did not forget that this was a full moon period. I was inside the house and I didn't know he had gone inside the chicken house at the back of the house. Next time I will be more careful. I am going to make sure this incident will never happen again."

Dada pricked up his ears at this and became more interested to find out the connection between the snake and the full moon period; but he had a major problem, which was that he could not ask any questions unless he was allowed to do so. So he looked away, pretending he was indifferent to all that was happening.

"There is not going to be a next time," said Ms Betika. "I don't want to see him here any more so his job is finished now. When I come back in the evening I don't want to see him. Understand!" Then Paul left.

Dada's teacher looked at Dada and said, "It is time for us to leave now. I am not going to get those girls. I only take them from school."

Dada asked himself, "What about the snake?" It was as though Ms Betika could only be communicated with by telepathy!

After Dada and his teacher started to leave, she said to him, "Don't worry about the snake incident. That was my auntie!"

Dada didn't know if he should laugh or take it seriously. He thought to himself, "If it is true that the snake is her auntie, how come she is a human being like me?"

"My auntie passed away the same day I was born," she explained to Dada. "It was during the full moon period. I was born when the earth energy was at its peak. It's a long story. Now my auntie appears in my house occasionally. I choose the chicken house because no-one goes there. She comes to visit me every time there is a full moon period. She appears every day at the same place between midday and two p.m. during the day, and between midnight and four o'clock in the morning. She is my protection against the evil spirits. I will teach you how to read the message in the sky. Here people can just look at the sky at any time for an explanation of what is happening, or predict what will happen. For example, next time it is getting cloudy or you think it will rain, just look at the sky. If the clouds are coming from that side of the N'sele area it is going to rain. You should be aware of where to be, but if the clouds come from a different direction, you don't need to be afraid because it will not rain; but if it rains it would be a dangerous rain and someone will have to die by thunder. There are some kinds of tree that you should not be next to at that moment, otherwise you will be killed by the thunder."

When they reached the school garden Dada was still puzzled. Ms Betika said to him, "My son, you must stop telling everybody about your background. Although they can tell you are not from here, you don't have to explain anything to anyone. Understand?"

"Yes Mum," replied Dada, and left to go to the classroom.

Chapter 10

At the end of the afternoon session Dada went to look for Bony again so they could go home together. He knew Bony would not refuse his friendship. After a few minutes he saw Bony leaving school alone and he said to him, "I was looking for you."

Why?" asked Bony.

"I have a lot to tell you—and don't worry about those people; they will stop annoying you if they see us together. So let's go—we have a lot to talk about."

"What lot of things to talk about?" asked Bony.

After a few minutes they started walking together like very good friends. Dada was very happy about the way things were turning out with Bony. They walked the same way where Dada was bullied. They didn't talk about the incident while walking together. When they reached their street, Dada stopped and said to Bony, "You know what, I went to Ms Betika's house today and what I saw there you wouldn't believe."

Bony was quiet, listening to what his friend was saying. Dada continued, "Before I tell you what I saw, I would like you to promise me you will not tell anyone."

"Who should I tell?" said Bony.

"You know, Ms Betika has a snake in her house that she calls her auntie."

"Is that what you want me not to tell anyone? That is for protection. Everyone has to protect oneself."

"What do you mean by everybody?" asked Dada.

"Don't tell me that your parents didn't give you anything before you came here!"

"Like what?" asked Dada

"Like something to protect yourself with. You know this place is very strange—you need some kind of protection."

"I was not given any protection, but I was given advice which can help me to enjoy this town. Also, I know how to pray. I have the photo of Saint Mary with baby Jesus and Pope Innocent III. I always pray in front of them in my room before I sleep. In my family we don't have a witch, and I don't want to be the first to have one!"

"I can show you how you can be popular everywhere you go," said Bony, "and also how to protect yourself. You know everyone here has some kind of protection against anything."

"Why don't you show me now?" said Dada.

"Tomorrow is Saturday. We have plenty of time on our hands to do whatever we want to do."

"I want something today."

"Okay, tomorrow is the day of sacrifice to the spirits of prosperity at the river. Not everyone is allowed to go, but I am—I'm special." He smiled. "No, I'm just joking! I know someone who can take us and we will be welcome there. I will come and take you to my master this evening."

"Where is the sacrifice going to take place?"

"At the place where the river Kabangu and Kwilu meet."

"Sylvan will not allow me to go that far."

"We can always say that we are going to watch football and he will let you come with me," said Bony.

"But what about tonight?" asked Dada. "What shall we tell him?"

"I will tell Sylvan that my mother sent me to collect something at her friend's house and he'll not ask any questions. I know that he will never allow you to play outside with us at night, so you wait for me—I'm coming back soon."

This was like the beginning of a long and exciting journey. Once inside the house Dada went straight to his room to get changed, then came outside to speak to Sylvan who was behind the house in the bungalow trying to tidy up the place.

"Sylvan, guess what?" said Dada.

"What is the big news?" said Sylvan.

"It's not really big news. It's just that Bony and me are talking. He said that he is coming to get me later on today to go with him to collect something."

"Okay, but don't stay at the people's place for long. Do you have any homework today?"

"No, I don't."

After that brief conversation Dada went inside the house to his room to sit and relax. At the same time he was trying to imagine himself with all this super-power and spiritual know-how. He was very impatient to find out what he was going to be exposed to that evening.

It was just a short while before Dada heard Sylvan calling his name. When he went outside he only saw Bony. "Where is Sylvan?" he asked.

"He said we can go and he has gone back behind the house," replied Bony, and added, "Let's go before he changes his mind!"

Chapter 11

They did not take a long time to arrive at the house of Joe Lumas, Bony's master. When they approached the door, Bony told his friend to remove his shoes. He did so. After that, Bony said aloud, "Master, master, it's me. I was just passing by and I would like to come and see you for a minute."

But no-one answered.

The compound in which Joe Lumas lived was actually his big sister's place. He had his small bungalow at the back of the main house where he lived alone. His sister worked at the Protestant Secondary School. He was the type of person who did not socialise much. He was always busy conducting ceremonies for different types of people, especially businessmen. After a short time Bony decided to go and ask at the main house; then they heard strange noises coming out of the Joe Lumas' house. Bony grabbed Dada's hand and they walked inside. Once inside the living room, Dada couldn't believe his eyes! He was so scared he almost wet his trousers. This was a big shock and he didn't know what to do. It was the first time in his life that he had come close to this kind of experience. He was traumatised and couldn't say anything. The place was in a complete mess—everything was on top of everything. The spirits were beating up Joe Lumas! Someone, quite invisible, was throwing him against the wall! They could hear voices but they couldn't see the people who were screaming—and it was getting dark.

Dada was convinced that he wouldn't leave that house alive and started asking himself, "Why did I come here?" He was scared and couldn't believe what he was seeing was really happening. The short time they were there seemed like hours to Dada. At one moment some kind of force appeared to lift Joe Lumas in the air, then let him go so that he collapsed badly. Dada could feel the pain! They stayed for a few minutes and he actually thought the man was dead. Just as he was trying to figure out what actually happened, Joe Lumas stood up and appeared very aggressive. He started coming slowly towards them, shouting, "Who are you? Who are you?"

Bony shouted back, "B.A.M....B.A.M...!" At that moment Bony spotted the danger and knew that he had to respond as quickly as possible, as Joe Lumas was now concentrating on Dada. Bony realised that his friend was in danger, and with both hands pulled out a cigarette called *Tumbacu* in his left hand, and a box of matches in his right hand; he always brought these with him when he came to see his master, for that cigarette is the most used during his ceremony. In a split second he lit the cigarette and gave it to Joe Lumas. The demented man stood in front of Dada and, when he put the cigarette in his mouth, he collapsed.

Bony said to Dada, "In this life you always need to be prepared for surprises."

They went to sit on the chair and Joe Lumas got up. He looked round and asked, "Bony, what happened here?"

Chapter 12

The next day, after school, Bony and Dada went to the ceremony that was taking place where the river Kabangu and the river Kwilu meet. The purpose of the ceremony was to appease the spirits of the river. In Bulungu, when something goes wrong, people always blamed themselves for annoying the spirits. The river ceremony was mainly organised by local businessmen, and even the Europeans took part on it. Women where not allowed during the proper ceremony, especially the hardcore inner circle of the organization, even if they were successful in their businesses. They could take part in the dancing and singing part, however, which was as far as they were permitted to be involved in the ceremony. It has been said that the spirits of the river propagated the female energy, so to receive the balance of energies, one needed to invite only men to participate in the function. Some people refused to buy that and stressed that this was yet another excuse for men to exclude women from an important ceremony that could affect their lives. But no one, man or woman, had ever challenged the status quo. For the people of this town, as long as casualties were prevented, no one cared to suggest otherwise.

When Dada and his friend arrived, the dancing and singing part had just finished. So most people who had nothing to do with the organisation were told to leave before the proper ceremony began.

Dada said to Bony, "We are late—the ceremony has just finished."

"No," replied his friend.

"Look," he said, "we are the only ones going toward the river."

"I know what I'm doing," said his friend. "Just follow me."

When they reached the place where the ceremony was taking place, Dada became frightened. His friend nevertheless appeared cool, as if nothing was happening.

Then Bony told Dada, "Wait for me here. I'm going to take part in the ceremony." He pointed. "Look," he continued, "there is Joe Lumas! I'm going to be with him. So you just stay here. Don't give the impression that you're not familiar with all this. Don't speak to anyone."

Dada had no alternative than to agree with his friend. He realised it was unwise to be where he was at that moment. He already started to think of lies to give to Ms Betika to justify his absence if she found out he did not go home straight away. While thinking about Ms Betika he heard a goat crying, "Meee, meee, meee…" Then he tried to look properly at what was happening to the goat. But he couldn't see what was really happening because people formed a circle, saying mysterious words he couldn't catch. He failed to grasp what they where doing. He could barely see the few people, four or five, that stood inside the circle formed by the crowd, holding what appeared to be a goat. He was not far from them but the visibility of the inner circle was not clear. He was standing roughly ten metres away from the circle, but, because there were so many people around the circle who were also agitated, it was difficult for him to see clearly what was happening.

Then he saw a man inside the circle holding the goat and a knife, and the rest of the people who were also holding the goat. The man with the knife was intoning certain words that Dada could not understand. In a split second blood was flowing out of the goat, splashing around, yet the goat was still alive! Then a few people carried the goat near the bridge, crossing the River Kabangu and threw the animal into the river as part of the ritual. The rest of the people who were taking part in the ritual carried on doing the same with the items they brought to the ceremony. Some brought boxes of salt fish, others brought boxes of soap, and also one tenth of their merchandise which they had to throw into the river to complete the ritual. It was said in Bulungu that if you could not please the spirit of the river, you would never prosper in business and you would never know how to manage your money properly—for the spirit of the river had a female energy. Dada was amazed. He was trying to make sense of it all and at the same time trying not to look like a complete novice to the ritual.

Just then a man came to him and said, "My name is Bazino—you must be Dada?"

"Yes," he responded, taken aback.

"Have you taken part in any spiritual ceremony before?" asked Bazino.

"Yes," Dada replied nervously. He didn't know what he would do if Bazino asked him anything that related to the spiritual world. He wouldn't know what to say and he would look like a liar, and such behaviour, he believed, was not tolerated in Bulungu. He wished someone would come and take Bazino away so he could have his peace.

Then a strange thing happened. Just as he wished, a man approached them. It was the man who was in charge of the ceremony. The man came close to Dada, standing in front of him and staring at him, while Dada stared at the ground.

The man said to Bazino, "Can you see what I can see coming out of this boy's face?"

"Yes, I can see," Bazino said.

Dada was frightened and did not know what to do. He thought he had been caught taking part in a ceremony he was not allowed to be in. He wished for the ground to open up and swallow him so that he would vanish. He was desperate to escape from a situation that was beyond his control.

Then the man spoke again to Bazino: "Are you sure you can see what is coming out of this boy's face?"

"Yes, Master," Bazino replied.

"No, you cannot see it," the man said again. "You shouldn't lie to me. I was just testing you because I know you are not trained to see what I'm talking about. I would like you to take this boy and make him a member and in a few weeks time you will thank me."

Dada didn't know what to say. He didn't know what they were talking about, but didn't dare to ask any questions. He was thinking they might make him a musician or an actor.

Then Bazino said to Dada, "Meet me tomorrow, after the morning mass. You should wait inside the Priest's garden, under the Mango tree, so that the person I send can find you easily."

Bazino and the man left and went to stand on the bridge to carry on taking part in the ceremony.

In the evening, Kabangu neighbourhood was always quiet. The only person who shouted up and down was Papa Simon telling people what the spirit had supposedly told him. As expected, tonight he appeared again, shouting and saying, "No children should go to the River Kabangu these days because there are crocodiles! And we all know what they are after! So no children in the river, no children, I really mean it!" He kept shouting this over and over, going up all the streets and repeating what he was saying, over and over.

Dada came to stand at the border of the property to see Papa Simon, and his friend Bony came to him and said, "Dada, I have something to ask you."

"Okay, why don't you come inside," he acquiesced.

They went into the back yard and sat on a piece of wood.

"I saw you talking with the Master," Bony said.

"Yes, but I didn't understand what he was telling me."

"What did he tell you?"

"If I can remember properly, he told the guy that was next to me..."

"Bazino?"

"How would I know his name?"

"Everybody knows Bazino. He is a man of many connections."

"The Master told him to make me a member. How would he do it?"

Then Bony started to laugh. "I knew you wouldn't understand what he was saying. I should go home now because it's getting late. Tomorrow I'll explain to you what he meant by being a member."

But Dada was impatient and kept insisting that Bony tell him.

"Okay," Bony said. "I'll tell you, but don't tell anyone I did, and when you meet Bazino, act as if you didn't know anything. Otherwise my life will be in danger!" He took a breath and continued: "Okay, being a member or a follower of Suroh, as they also say, is not what you would imagine. A 'member' is a member of a secret order called *Etoile d'oree* (Golden Star) and they love calling themselves *les adeptes de Suroh* (the followers of Suroh), but never tell anyone that I told you this because this order officially does not exist; nobody knows about it except the members. The order is still in its formation process."

"Well, how do you know?" Dada asked. "Are you also a member?"

"That's a bad habit for someone who wants to be a 'member' to have. It's bad to start asking question before you even know what it's all about. It's going to be very different from what you expect. I don't know much about what the order stands for myself. I was told it was created primarily as a club of Catholic pupils from Bulungu who will one day defend their faith around the World. That will also be their fraternity club and girls are not allowed. What Joe Lumas, who is a Protestant, told me was that they are creating a secret fraternity for their own purposes, but no-one else, beside the creators, really knows what the club is all about. They already have members who are in boarding school, such as *Petit Seminaire De Kinzambi* and the *Institut De Fraternite* (Institute of Brotherhood) in Kikwiti, shortened to *Infran*."

"I have heard of the *fraternite* before," said Dada.

"Where did you hear about it?"

"I am not sure," Dada replied, "but I know a place in Kinshasa called the centre of *Olympia La Fraternite*. My father used to go there a lot."

"Let's go to my place," said Bony. "I have to give you some of the things you need to have so you can start your journey in the spiritual world as smoothly as possible."

Before they left Dada asked the permission of the houseboy if he could go to Bony's house and he was allowed to do so, but just for a short time. When they were about to leave Dada's house, they heard Papa Simon again shouting to warn people about the danger of the crocodiles' presence in the River Kabangu. Then Bony whispered to Dada, "I have something to tell you, but don't tell anyone."

Dada was excited to find out what other people didn't know. "Who would I tell if it is not you," he said. "You are my only best friend, and if I don't tell you I don't have anyone else to tell."

"Okay, I believe you," Bony said. "Just watch in a few days—Papa Simon will either be killed or beaten up seriously, because many people who have strong connections with the spiritual world are upset with him, even some Kabangu residents. They're not happy with what he is doing."

Dada was surprised and asked, "Why should people be upset with him if he is preventing the deaths of many people?"

"It's not the same way as you think of it," Bony said. "Many people in this place, especially in this neighbourhood, depend on spiritual protections for their everyday lives. When something happens to them they believe they are being bewitched. So to overcome that obstacle they have to go to see someone who specialises in lifting the spell. But since Papa Simon came the population became dependant on him because he tells them if there is a foreign crocodile in the river or not; thus people simply make a decision as to whether to go to the river or not rather than seek protection against the crocodiles. So that is why he is going to be killed soon. I even know the people who are going to do it, and they are just waiting for the football game that will take place on Wednesday afternoon: they will attack him if he comes to watch the game. With that confusion nobody, including the police, will know who did what. It will just appear as an accident."

Dada felt sorry for Papa Simon but what could he do? Nothing! When they started to leave for Bony's house, they literally passed close to Papa Simon who was still shouting. Dada looked at him and felt sorry that the man's days were numbered. He felt helpless, not being able to do anything about the man who in his eyes had done nothing wrong. But he also felt important, knowing what only few people knew. When they reached Bony's house he asked his friend, "With me joining the *Etoile d'oree* club, is there anything they will stop me from doing?"

"The only thing they will tell you is that you are defending the faith and you are part of a network of people who have been studying in this Primary school before, who are very intelligent and who are being prepared for one day when they will take high offices in the capital; they will act as good Catholics and also help their brothers; but you should never reveal your membership to anyone who is not a member. Anyway, you can never be a full member while you are still in Primary school. While you are still at Primary school they are just initiating you to know more about the club. It is only when you leave and go to a boarding school or go to join your family in America, maybe, that they would make you a full member. There will be certain things you can never do again, and you will never tell your parents that you are a member. You are going to be given a yellow rosary that has only ten beads. You will have to keep it in your pocket and also a picture of your Patron Saint, to keep with you all the time, and you will use it for your prayers. It will be good if they trust you. That will make them tell you more about the club. I also share with you what I know about what Joe Lumas always tell me, so we can combine our knowledge to do something very exciting. In this town children always pretend to their parents to be innocent, although some of them know a lot about the spiritual world. Most of the children, between the ages of ten to twelve, have what is called special prayers to the spirits which they can use in times of need."

Bony told Dada to wait for him outside the house, and he went inside and returned with a copybook. "Let's go to your place," he said to. When they reached Dada's house they were about to go to Dada's bedroom when the surprised houseboy asked Bony, "Don't you think it's a bit late for you to be here now instead of being at home?" Bony replied that they had homework that he needed Dada to explain to him, an explanation that satisfied the houseboy.

They went into Dada's bedroom and sat on the edge of the bed. When Bony opened the book he was carrying, he took out another book that was inside the first book. When he opened it Dada noticed the papers of the tiny book were parchment papers.

"What do you need all this parchment paper for?" Dada asked his friend.

"That's what you will be using to write prayers. Not any kind of prayers, I mean, magical prayers that will enable you to do anything to anyone at any time; but you shouldn't show them to anyone. People will find it acceptable and normal for you to have these prayers, but you shouldn't tell them that you have them. Also, never ever let a girl or any woman touch it! Once they do so, it would cause the magical power of the prayers to vanish. Women are very powerful, you know, but they don't know. If they know what they had they would overtake everything, so it is better that way. Never ever let them even see it. But those prayers I am going to give you, you cannot take it for free. That's the way it works. You need to pay something for it. That is to prevent someone stealing them and trying to use them. These prayers can only work once you pay something. I will show you how to use it, which kind of perfume to use, which powder and which kind of candles you would need to use for your rituals. We call these prayers 'numbers'. You have numbers for almost everything, but I won't give you everything today. I will let you copy only three numbers. One is to make someone forgetful, another is for domination, and the last one is for your own protection against bad spells. Then you will pay me when you have finished copying them. I will leave the book with you, so you can copy them in your own time."

Dada didn't know what to do. He was happy that he was getting all this information, but at the same time he was also concerned about what would happen to him when his family knew about the numbers. He asked, "Is there any visible change that will happen to me when I start practising these prayers?"

"No," said Bony, "not really. It's only the ones I am going to give you next time—the ones I received from Joe Lumas. That would be traditional ones. I'm going to give you the power to be strong physically and to divert thunder when someone sends it to you. But the only thing I would stop you doing would be eating the head of a fish, and running when it is raining."

Dada felt confused and wondered if this was what he really wanted to do. He asked why he should not eat the head of a fish and run when it was raining.

"The head of a fish is what is used as an ingredient for some of the power I would give you; if you eat it, it will spoil everything. Also, when it is raining and you are running at the same time, you would upset the spirits that send the thunder. Your life has to be around water. From now on, water should be sacred for you."

After that, Bony left and told Dada not to copy the prayers today and to leave them for later, since those kind of prayers could only be copied when the sun was out.

CHAPTER 13

▼

Outside the school the boy was becoming confused about who he was and what his responsibilities were. He was afraid of what might happen to him if he did not follow the rules given by any Master who would initiate him into the spiritual world. But although he felt sorry for Papa Simon regarding what was about to happen to him, he saw himself as very privileged to know what only a few people were permitted to know in Bulungu. That privileged status was pushing him to know more and to be initiated into anything that he could come across. His life was becoming a mixture of feelings. He was sad for the long absence of his guardian, yet also happy that he could do anything he liked. In only a short time he had noticed the cohabitation of beliefs or faiths in the inhabitants. One could simultaneously be a practising Christian and openly pagan. People of Bulungu were very tolerant on this matter. But when it came to Christian faith, no-one was expected to be Protestant and Catholic at the same time. No-one would do you harm if you chose to be so, but you would be condemned on both sides and that might even cost you your friends. They might still talk to you but no longer as intimate friends. At the markets you would be a laughing stock from both sides.

As a young person it was a risky adventure to try and embrace both faiths. You could get into lots of trouble. Verbal or physical abuse would be your everyday companion. You could also be bullied if you went to a separate Church than that of your parents, or went to a school that was not part of your parents' faith. So far it was only Dada who could get away with such things as himself being a Catholic while his guardian was a Protestant. No-one was giving him a hard time for that. In that sector, he could call himself an untouchable. When he got bad treatment among the boys of his age he always thought of it as a result of jealously because of the way he dressed. That's why, since the departure of his guardian, he no longer liked to wear nice clothes—In order to try to integrate into the town. There were times when the boys even laughed at him, telling him something like, "Don't try too much, you can never be one of us!" That always used to make him feel sad for a short time. It was only Bony, Dada often thought to himself, who was his true friend and who understood him. "I will take him to see my parents when they come back from America," he mused. He did not look forward to moving back with his family. Indeed, he started to despise the way he had been brought up. The idea of one day moving back with them was becoming irksome and started to become his nightmare. When he looked back to where he came from he couldn't believe how he had survived it. Being protected by military bodyguards twenty-four hours a day and not being able to have proper friends and play with them, now appeared to him as synonymous with death itself. "No, I am going nowhere and I will live here forever," he told himself from time to time. His enjoyment of staying in Bulungu invariably faded every evening when he realised that he was the only one with no proper family. For some reason Sylvan didn't talk to him very much either. Sometimes he was left alone in the evenings so Sylvan could go and do his own things. And so Dada was left to live the life of two opposite feelings at the same time.

Besides the pupils, for the rest of the population of Bulungu going to Church was not compulsory. Hardly anyone went to Mass on Sunday—even those who used to brag about their faith. But this Sunday was a special one for the Catholic residents of Bulungu. There was going to be a service that would be conducted by two visiting and famous priests. Their celebrity had nothing to do with the fact of how well they represented the person who replaced St Peter as the head of the Church or how close they were to the Curia in Rome. Nevertheless they were much loved just because they were Zairians. One would hear young Catholics saying to their Protestant counterparts, "If you think we are useless, what about those priests?"

All Catholic parents were making sure that they would attend the service with their children. There were rumours that even some Protestants were planning to be there too. The local priest held a meeting with the Community Leaders and some teachers to co-ordinate the event, because people would also have to come from the nearby villages.

The starting time for the service was pushed back to nine o'clock in the morning, but by six a.m. people were already sitting on the grass of the Churchyard. Some were feeding their children or talking to one another about the service, while others were singing. There were no topics to the conversations other than the Papacy.

Besides the known special days of their Church such as Good Friday, Easter, etc., this was the fourth time the people of Bulungu were gathered for a special service in less than four months. The first one was to mourn the death of Pope Paul VI; the second was to celebrate the choice of Pope John Paul I as his successor. The whole of the population was shocked when they were called to mourn the death of a newly elected Pope. Perhaps that was why this time the Cardinal and his aids had chosen those two loved Priests to go around to let people know that there were no curses in the Church, and also to celebrate the election of Pope John Paul II. They were handing leaflets and postcards of Pope Paul VI, Pope John Paul I and Pope John Paul II with the printed message at the back, each respectively saying:

- Pope Paul VI: real name Giovani Battista Montini, born at Concescio near Brescia in Italy on 26th September 1897. Ordained on 29th May 1920. Appointed Archbishop of Milan on 1st November 1954. Became Pope on 21st June 1963 and died, after suffering a heart attack, on 6th August this year at Castle Ciandolfo in Italy.

- Pope John Paul I: Real name Albino Luciani, born on 17th October 1912 at Forno Di Canale near Belluno in Italy. Ordained as a priest on 7th July 1935. Appointed Bishop of Vittono Veneto in Italy in December 1958 by Pope John XXIII. Became Cardinal on 5th March 1973. Became Pope on 26th of last August and died three weeks later after his inauguration on Thursday 28th September of this year of heart attack while lying in his bed.

- Pope John Paul II: Real name Karol Wajtyla. Born on 18th May 1920 at Wadowice, Poland. Ordained as a priest in August 1946. Became Bishop on 4th July 1958, Archbishop on 30th December 1963 and Cardinal on 26th June 1967 and elected Pope on 16th October this year.

At eight o'clock in the morning, when the door of the Church opened, people rushed inside as if they were being chased by the Presidential Guards who were notorious for dispersing anti-Government rallies. All the children were well dressed and accompanied by their parents except Dada. On his arrival at the Churchyard, Dada immediately went into the building. He could barely see an empty seat, so he decided to walk to the front of the congregation, thinking he might find an empty seat there. Because he was walking by himself, it was easy for Ms Betika to notice him. She sent one of her pupils to call him. The Mass was uplifting for Dada. At the end of it he was able to talk to people, but still had a serious concern. He could see Bony with his parents but could not join them. He did not know how to break away from Ms Betika in order to keep his important rendezvous in the Church garden. At the same time, Ms Betika felt obliged to help the boy not feel lonely. Dada was very curious to be part of the secret club and felt privileged to be chosen to become a member. He would know a lot of things that only a few people knew. Also, it would satisfy his curiosity. But Ms Betika did not want to leave him by himself. Dada felt as if his life was being demolished! Things even went from bad to worse when he heard her saying to someone, "We are now going home because I have a lot of things to do," and she grabbed Dada by his hand so they could go. Once at Ms Betika's house, they had lunch. After that she told Dada to go back home. By that time Dada had already missed his rendezvous in the Church garden. He began to walk home disconsolately, but then decided to go straight to Bony's house instead of his own.

"Where were you?" Bony said as soon as he saw him. "They were looking for you!"

"You know where I've been," Dada said.

"That's not what we should talk about now," Bony advised. "I have a few things for you to keep, given to me by Bazino. Okay, let me go and get them from my house."

In a short time Bony came back with a brown envelope which he gave to Dada and told him, "No one should see what is inside, even me. I shouldn't see it, but the way I know it you don't need to break any rules. If you do break those rules I won't be able to help."

Dada panicked and said to his friend, "These are supposed to be Church matters—so why does it have so many rules to obey?"

But his friend didn't answer him. Silence fell over them. Dada broke the silence and said, "Okay, what I would need to do now is to protect myself."

"No—not again," Bony replied. "I'm too tired to do anything today." Bony understood what his friend had asked him, so he just kept on shaking his head, saying, "No, no, no."

Dada remained calm. In a few seconds, Bony relented. "Okay, let us go to your house first so that Sylvan sees you; then we can go to Joe Lumas for your protection."

Once they reached Joe Lumas' place they saw him sitting in the front of his small house. He knew directly what they needed because at that time during the day Bony and Dada would never come to see him unless Bony needed a favour.

He said to Bony, "Okay, I'm going to help your friend. You guys can pay me later."

They went inside the house and he told Dada to remove his shirt while Bony sat next to him. He performed his rituals so he would be ready to be in contact with the spirits. After a while he stopped and said to them, "You know, I don't get customers for this kind of protection since this stupid guy came into this Town."

"Do you mean Papa Simon?" Bony asked.

"Yes, that's him, that stupid guy," Joe Lumas said. "Since he came into this town people don't come to us for protection anymore. So the only way we can secure our livelihood is to get rid of him!" After that he started performing his ritual again. He brought a bottle of water, told Dada to open his mouth and poured it into his mouth whilst reciting certain incomprehensible words. At the end he told Dada, "This is the water from the Mediterranean Sea. From now on, you possess the spirit of water. Nothing can happen to you while you are swimming in the river. Any river or sea would become sacred to you. To get in touch with the spirits of water, you need to go near any river and stare at it for a while. You will see for yourself what will happen to you." Afterwards, he used a razor to cut small wounds in Dada's arms and put some powder into the wounds, and said, "This is to make you a very strong person at night and to protect you from anyone's attack, and from any animal in the forest that tries to kill you. Now, I am going to do the last one." Then he left them inside the house, went out and returned carrying a live chicken. He told Bony to hold the chicken. While the chicken was looking at them, he used a sharp knife to chop its head off. The head jumped off and bounced around his small living room and blood splattered everywhere. Then Joe Lumas held the chicken's neck securely and placed it close to Dada so the blood could spread on his face. He told Dada to rub the blood in properly.

After completing this part of the ritual, he said to Dada, "This is as far as I can go today. So I am finished. You must give Bony what he tells you to give him so that all these things will start working on you."

When they finished, Dada began to have mixed feelings and started asking himself if it was really a good thing to be doing what he was doing. He started to wonder whether he was creating more problems than solving any. But he didn't want his friend to see him as a coward, so he pretended everything was fine, although he was scared stiff. He didn't want to go home with blood on his face. He used his shirt to wipe off the blood and his shirt became red. Then they left. He couldn't wear his shirt anymore.

When they reached his house, he pretended he had just come in from playing football. With his shirt in his hand, he went straight into his bedroom and put the shirt under the bed where Sylvan wouldn't find it. He knew very well that Sylvan would ask questions if he saw the shirt in that state. He would need to find a way of washing it before Sylvan got hold of it. He decided he would have to go to the river with his friends. He knew that he was not allowed to do so, but that was the only way he could wash it.

Later that day, in the evening, when Dada was sitting with Sylvan, they heard the bells of both Churches, Protestant and Catholic, start to ring. At first Dada did not pay attention as he thought it was to do with the Church services. It was only when they heard the noise of gunfire and Sylvan said "Not again," that Dada realised something was wrong. So he asked Sylvan, "What's wrong? What's happening?"—for Dada had become confident of asking any questions.

"Someone is dead by accident," Sylvan replied. "Maybe in the river. I hope it's not to do with the crocodiles again."

"By a crocodile?" said Dada.

"It's a long story," Sylvan said. "But to cut a long story short, you always need to be very careful every time you go to swim in the river. By the way, it's not important because you wouldn't go to the river by yourself. The way the bells kept on ringing it seemed to me that the accident concerned more than one person—maybe a dreadful one."

After a short silence, Sylvan said to Dada, "I know you do not have any protection against the witches of this town, so you need to be very careful."

Dada almost smiled but kept calm so as not to arouse any suspicion. He remembered that he had heard stories about crocodiles in school, especially from his friend Bony, but never paid any attention to them. So he asked Sylvan, "What's wrong with the crocodiles?"

Sylvan hesitated. "You see, Dada, you need to be very careful in this town. The river could be very dangerous; but you don't have anything to worry about because you can only go to the river when Mr Masa is around. Also, I need to be there, as before, when you play or swim with your friends. But never go with anyone else, because they all have protection against any evil spirit of the river—but you don't."

Hearing that, Dada immediately felt the need to go to the river with his friends since he knew he had some kind of protection. Sylvan managed to switch to a different subject, telling Dada about his village and some myths that were passed on to them from generation to generation, and Dada enjoyed them. After a short while Bony came to join them. Sylvan left to let the boys get on with their lives. So he went into the house to close the windows to avoid mosquitoes coming inside, and also to light up the oil lamp. Dada took the opportunity to ask Bony again about the crocodiles at the river, and Bony explained it all to him. He concluded by saying, "That's why my Master and his friends don't like Papa Simon. They cannot earn a living any more. That's why something should happen to him, so they can get back their customers."

Dada sat there, speechless, and Bony said again, "Before I just came to your place now I overhead Thomas' mother telling my mum that four girls of the same family have just died in Kabangu River."

"How?" asked Dada, aghast.

"I don't know, we will find out tomorrow in school."

After three days, on Wednesday, there were many people in the stadium of Bulungu for a big match between two rival football teams, known as AS Kivuvu and FC Virunga. On Wednesdays the children didn't have to go back for the afternoon session at school, which was why the Bulungu Football Association always chose Wednesday as a day for big games. Usually the kick-off took place at 4 p.m.

Even before the game started the mood was tense, although it was just a friendly match. Throughout the game, the two teams found it difficult to score and everyone expected a draw. Just a few minutes before the end of the match the referee accorded a penalty to AS Kivuvu and immediately the fans of FC Virunga contested it. At first it started as a reasonable and legitimate argument between fans and players of both sides. But in the end it all degenerated into total chaos. All who knew they could not hold a fight chose running away as the only option. But for Dada everything was different. When he arrived at the stadium he went with his friend Bony to establish Papa Simon's whereabouts. Everyone was trying to find a place to stand and when the fight broke out Dada, again, risked his life to seek out Papa Simon where he was standing. He saw him walking slowly away from the pitch. He also saw a few guys walking behind him, as if they were among those people who did not believe in violence as a means of solving problems. Dada, alone this time, also walked innocently next to them just to see what would happen. Although he was told by his friend Bony about the conspiracy against Papa Simon, he did not fully believe it. He did not want to look suspicious to people around Papa Simon, so he kept his distance. From where Dada was it looked as though one of the guys had called Papa Simon's name. Then Dada saw Papa Simon with all confidence turning back to see who was calling his name. For Dada the events unfolded as if in a dream. He saw one of the guys produce an empty glass bottle and smash it against Papa Simon's head. With just a single blow on his head, Papa Simon collapsed to the ground. Like a magnetic effect, some people nearby converged towards the poor man. To Dada it looked as if they were going to kill him. He rushed to the spot to satisfy his curiosity and shouted, "What's happening? What's happening?" Before he even got close to where he was going he was stopped by a slap on the face by a person he didn't even see. He collapsed and for an instant everything turned black. Then he became aware of blood coming from his nose. He quickly got up and ran away to safety.

Chapter 14

The following Saturday, Bony with his friends arranged to go to Kabangu River. Dada asked Bony if he could join them. Bony said, "No problem." Dada disregarded what Sylvan told him because he knew he had to wash his bloodstained shirt before it could be noticed by anyone. After he came home from school, he saw Sylvan sitting at the front of the house.

"What are you going to do this afternoon?" Sylvan asked.

"I'm going to play football with my friends," Dada replied.

So Dada went into the house, to his bedroom, to take the bloodied shirt from under his bed to hide it properly; then came back outside and said to Sylvan, "I'm off to play football with Bony and the rest of the boys." In a short while he met up with Bony and the rest of the boys and they made their way to the river. Dada had nothing to be afraid of because he knew he also had protections, just like the other boys. So he went off with confidence.

Once they reached the river Dada went straight to the edge of the riverbank while all the boys stayed further back. They began to take off their clothes as they would have to swim across the river to play football on the other side.

Dada started to play with some stones, trying to throw them and make them skim across the top of the water. He was showing off that he was the best and soon Bony joined him, saying, "I will always beat you at this game!"

Dada turned away from the river and bent down to find the best stones to compete with Bony. He heard the boys who were still further away begin to shout: "Dada, Dada!"—and he turned to look. At the same time Bony looked at Dada to find out why they other boys were calling him. Then he saw the big crocodile coming up behind Dada from the river. He knew that if he shouted

Dada's name it would be too late. So instead he ran towards Dada and pushed him out of the way while he was still trying to stand up, causing him to fall to the side. At the same time, while he was pushing Dada, the crocodile swung its tail from left to right so it could knock over its victim—and Bony was the unlucky one, the tail of the crocodile smashing him right in his face. He collapsed, half of his body in the river. The noise of Bony falling into the river distracted the crocodile from Dada. It turned its attention to Bony instead, capturing the boy and drawing him deeper into the water while all his friends looked on helplessly.

Dada could not believe his eyes! He was sitting just a short distance from where this was all happening, but he didn't move, he didn't scream, even though all the boys were screaming for him to get away before the crocodile came back. He just continued to sit and stare at the spot where Bony had been just a few seconds before. The water had rapidly turned red with Bony's blood.

All the boys ran away as if the crocodile were pursuing them, leaving Dada by himself. Only one of the boys realised that Dada was not with them and came back to see what had happened to him. He saw Dada still sitting in the same place and asked him, "Dada, are you okay?"

Dada did not answer him. The friend said again, "It's me, Lama."

Dada was still quiet, so Lama grabbed him forcibly in his hands and pulled him away from the scene. Before they reached home Dada realised what had happened and started to cry. Lama said to him, "No, don't cry, it's not your fault." Dada kept on crying and said, "It *was* my fault! It was because he tried to help me. I was the one who started to play that game. That's why he's dead!"

"Don't worry," Lama said. "We are all still here, we are all still your friends. There will be no problem, it will all be resolved."

He took Dada to his house. The weather was dry. The sun was making its apparent journey into the darkness. It was not too hot but the calm that the boys found in the neighbourhood gave Dada a bad feeling. Sylvan was not at home and Dada went straight into his bedroom to sleep. He could not believe what had happened. He still thought he was dreaming and that when he woke up everything would be all right. He had heard of crocodiles before, but never thought he would see one so close to him. Even if he saw one, he never believed it would be in such a frightening way. He tried to cry aloud but still didn't feel any better. He knew that even if crying was appropriate at that moment it would still not change anything. "What has happened?" he asked himself. "*Why* did I come to this town? Why did my parents have to send me here? What will I do now? What's happened to my only best friend could easily have happened to me!" He kept tormenting himself with such questions. He was surprised that no church bells had yet rung for Bony. There were no people crying from the neighbourhood, nor anyone on the streets. He felt exhausted, as if he had not slept for many days. With all that had happened to him, he could still not believe he was actually still alive.

The accident had made Dada understand what life could offer. It forced him to become a grown-up straightaway. Yet he didn't know how to face the world after the loss of his friend. He felt as though he had a sharp pain in his heart and again he started to blame himself for failing to obey Sylvan.

He reviewed everything that had happened lately and he started to correct his every action in his mind. But he realised there was little he could do. "Bony is dead in the river," he kept on saying to himself. "Why me! Why am I here?"

With the death of the four girls from the same family, Papa Simon in a coma in the Central Hospital and now Bony captured by the crocodile, Dada, with his new knowledge of the spiritual world, believed the town had been cursed. When he thought of the protection he had sought he became even more scared. He did not know what to do with all the material he had been given so far. He would like to give it back, but what about those inside his body? When he reached that point he felt sick. He still felt guilty of the death of his friend. He did not care even if all the windows of the house were closed and the room was dark. What was important to him was what would happen to him afterwards. He knew from now his life would never be the same again. After a short time he fell asleep, exhausted from the futile attempt to correct all the recent actions of his life within his mind.

He did not hear both the bells of the two Churches when they started to ring and the gunfire. He was in a deep sleep. He was woken up by the noise of the people shouting inside their compound and also by the noise that sounded like big stones being thrown on the roof. He almost forgot what had happened. At first he thought he had slept for two nights consecutively. He heard the noise getting louder and louder, still not knowing what the people were saying. Then he tried to open the window to see what was really happening. He heard someone shouting, "He's in, let's kill him! He's a killer and he doesn't deserve to live!" He closed the window quickly and started asking himself what he was going to do! He became convinced that he was going to be killed! He could hear the big stones bouncing off the window and also someone trying to break down the front door of the house. He started to shake and knew there was no point trying to hide. He sensed that today was his last day to live. He just sat on the edge of the bed, his body shaking with fear. He could hear the door being shaken and heard it collapse, but still he did not move. The house was dark and the people who broke the door down appeared to have a torch. He could hear them shouting, "Where are you, where are you?"—but he did not answer. His shaking became more pronounced and uncontrolled. When he realised that the light was coming towards his bedroom he just closed his eyes. He could not see how many people were coming inside the room. He didn't want to witness his own death.

The arrival of the inhabitants of Kabangu neighbourhood and Bony's relatives in his house, to cause trouble and to seek revenge for the death of their boy that Dada had supposedly pushed in the water, did not come as a surprise to Sylvan. When he came across the news of Bony's death and Dada's probable involvement on it, he knew what would be the consequences. He was aware of what would happen to both of them. This was the reason why he did not wake Dada up when he came home and found him sleeping, and why he just went outside again, locked the door with a key and ran away for his own safety. He was disappointed with Dada, but there was no time for a moral lecture now or even to wake the boy up.

Heaven only knew what would happen to both of them if those people came to find him and Dada at home. So in that particular moment, he believed he was left with no other alternative than to run away from the house. He chose not to go to his parents' house in case they came to look for him there. Instead, he went straightaway to one of his cousins who lived in N'Sele, a working class neighbourhood located in the far south-east end of the town. Once he arrived there he briefed his cousin and instructed him to dispatch someone to his parents' house so they, too, could run for their lives. He assumed no one among the inhabitants of Kabangu neighbourhood would actually break into the house. Once they found out the door was locked, he believed, they would go away. Certainly—so he convinced himself—they would believe that the boy had run away with him. So they would have to go to his parents' house in pursuit of them both.

For Dada much had changed in a very short time. Only days before he was a much-loved boy who was welcomed into the big family, and now he turned out to be public enemy number one! If they realised, thought Sylvan, that the supposed killer of Bony was not to be found, they would just go and mourn their dead boy and call off their search. But life, especially in Bulungu, did not always go as planned. The people in Bulungu could be as unpredictable as the weather. At the time he thought the people would be heading to his parents' house he gave his cousin the key to Mr. Masa's house so he could go and rescued Dada, warning him to be cautious.

The presence of people inside Mr. Masa's compound came to no surprise to Sylvan's cousin. What surprised him was the number and range of instruments they were carrying with them. He could also see from where he was standing that some passersby's seemed to enjoying the show, and that no one among those passersby's was publicly expressing a different opinion from those of the people who were inside the compound. He could sympathise with those people, who had lost their son, but this was not the time to take sides—he had a mission to accomplish. As he realised he could not possibly rescue Dada, Sylvan's cousin decided to execute 'Plan B.'

The arrival of the news of Bony's demise in the form of the church bells ringing reached Ms Betika in her own house. It had been a custom for a long time for the people of Manzanza neighbourhood, another working-class neighbourhood near the confluence of the rivers Kabungu and Kwilu, that when the church bells rang to announce someone's death, the inhabitants leave their houses, line up on the streets as a sign of respect and, of course, establish the identity of the person who had died. Ms Betika, as part of her integration process in that neighbourhood, had always come out of her compound when the bells rang. Sometimes she even went to the Church to find out for her herself. Then she could bring back the accurate information to the neighbourhood. This time she was preparing her notes for Monday's class. She got up when the bells started to ring to go and see what was happening. She didn't really want to go outside her compound to get involved in all the talking with the neighbours. She just went out as a formality so they would see her and one of them would say, "Oh, look, she's still one of us—she's out again to talk to us and to get involved with the community." That would probably be followed by the response: "What's wrong with this town, do people enjoy dying or what? Do you have a clue who is dead, Ms Betika?"—and she would answer them, merely for the sake of formality so she would appear to be connected with them. After that she would understand that their questions were their way of politely asking her to go to the Church to find out what was happening. She would reply, before leaving, "Let me go to see the priest and find out who is dead."

But this time she wasn't in the mood for leaving her house and she was reluctant to interrupt her work. She merely came out so she could go back in as quickly as possible and carry on with her work. Once she was outside of her compound she avoided eye contact with the people on the streets who were talking to each other to understand what was going on, and she began to return without delay. But just as she was walking back she heard someone on the streets saying, "It's one of those Catholic boys…He has been killed in Kabangu river this afternoon." She immediately turned back to ask the young woman who was propagating the news to repeat what she was saying. The woman said, "I did not verify it but I don't think those people who told me just now near the Church could lie to me." Ms Betika asked if she knew the identity of the boy who was killed, and it was only then that the woman answered in the affirmative, saying, "Yes, yes. I think they said his name was Dada. Yes, I think so. His name must be Dada."

Then, to everybody's surprise, Ms Betika jumped like an antelope that had unexpectedly met a lion in the forest. She ran not in the direction of the Church but towards the so-called 'Ville' neighbourhood that was situated near the river Kwilu.

The Ville was an upper-class neighbourhood where all the representatives of the Central Government lived. The Europeans had lived in the neighbourhood since colonial times. Some wealthy local merchants also chose the area as a place to build their big houses, thanks to independence, before which the region used to be a 'no go' area for the locals, wealthy or not—one would be breaking the law by going there (with some exceptions, for those who worked there as housekeepers, gardeners or human carriers).

When she arrived in the Ville area Ms Betika went directly to the District Judge's house. Once there, she was let inside the compound with no fuss or delay. She went into the Judge's garden and saw him drinking the local beer with the District Prosecutor. Both were from Kasai Province and appointed by the Central Government.

"You know," said the Judge to Ms Betika, "you don't have to be stressed every time. Come and join us."

"What do you mean by saying I should not be stressed?" Ms Betika asked, and she added, while still standing, "Don't you know it's our responsibility to organise the funeral?"

"Sit down," said the Prosecutor. "Let me call the houseboy to bring you a glass."

They were both half drunk and jovial at the time Ms Betika came to speak to them. While the Prosecutor was talking to Ms Betika the Judge was laughing for no apparent reason. It was only when she said to them, "How can you guys be so irresponsible and insensitive? How can you two be sitting here, happily drinking, when the Ambassador's son has just been killed by his friends?"

They both jumped up from their seats and shouted, "No, no!"—for they knew instantly to whom she was referring. The Judge's wife and some people who were in the house came out running towards the garden where her husband was sitting with his friend. She started to scream, "Bring a dry stick, bring a dry stick," thinking her husband or his friend had been attacked by a snake in the garden. When the people thus hastily summoned reached the Judge they soon realized there was no snake!

The Judge did not live with his children who used to go to boarding schools, even the youngest who was only six years old. That was a common practice among upper-class parents or those who wanted to joint the club of the privileged of the regime.

The news of Dada's death hit them hard, especially the Judge's wife who had always been against the idea of children being sent away from their parents to get some sort of real education. When she was with her friends, she always said, "Why one should teach innocent kids not to express their feelings, I'll never understand. It's turning them into robots!" But whatever she thought or said to her friends, she knew she could never repeat her opinions in front of her husband for fear of being thrown out of the house.

The noise of the Judge's wife made the neighbours hasten to find out what was happening. All the women who came joined the Judge's wife in crying, though their husbands stood with the rest of the men discussing the funeral arrangements and choosing the person who would be in charge of contacting the boy's parents. The place was like a circus. The Judge's wife started to roll about on the grass, leading the rest of the women in crying. Even some European women started to cry about the boy who, until that day, they didn't even know existed. Some of them may have heard of his father in the national news, but it would almost be impossible for them to know about the boy since he was supposed to be kept at a low profile in Bulungu.

For Bantu people who lived in Bulungu, it was women who cried at funerals while their husbands were supposed to be quiet. It was common knowledge that a woman who resisted crying at a funeral would be treated with suspicion, even if she didn't know the deceased. She might be a witch or might even have something to do with the person's death. So women always cried in any funeral, especially, too, because they were considered creatures of passion in every sense. For this reason Bantu people in Bulungu were more afraid of female witches than male witches.

But when one saw a man in a funeral crying aloud, it was always considered a sign of desperation. They didn't expect a man to have any passion. It was also said that when a man cried at a funeral it meant he was destitute and did not have any money on him. People were well advised to leave him alone, or do no more than ask who he was. If he was a head of the family, it meant he was asking for help, to encouraging others to contribute by giving money so he would be able to bury the dead body. Or, if he was not related to the dead person, his sad demeanor was to elicit pity and make people feel sorry for him. Since he didn't have any money to contribute to the funeral expenses, no one would be likely to be hard on him. At least he cried. After all, death might hit his family as well, so it was in his interests to display grief—or so he might have argued.

After a short time the Prosecutor, with the Judge's consent, sent one of his bodyguards to go to the Presidential Mansion, which was commonly referred to by the Bulungu residents as the 'Residence', to fetch ten soldiers among those stationed there so justice could be done to those who supposedly killed Dada. He even went so far as to shout so everyone could hear and would know who had the real power in Bulungu. He concluded by saying to his bodyguard, "If there are any problems, contact me on my Motorola and, I repeat again, I want all the boys to be arrested and brought to the Police Station where they will spend the night. Anyone who interferes should be arrested too. Tell the soldiers to take their weapons with them as well." Then he continued: "I shall see them tomorrow in my office and the Judge will deal with them tonight. For you," he said again to his bodyguard, "I'm going to spit on the ground and I want you to be back before it dries! Tell them to take four Land Rovers to have some space for those useless boys, and don't forget your Motorola as well!" By saying Motorola the Prosecutor meant walkie-talkie, which was because Motorola was the favoured brand used by the Government. The distance between the Judge's house and the Residence was just about half a kilometre.

The way the Judge's wife was crying started to annoy her husband. The mention of their children's name in her crying maddened him and he began to make his way towards her. He had to be held back by a neighbour who said to him, "We have more important issues to deal with now!" He called the Judge's driver to get the Land Cruiser Jeep ready to drive the Judge to the Police Station so he could question those boys tonight. He also said, "You two"—pointing at the Judge's bodyguards—"Get yourself ready to go with your boss." And the Judge with Ms Betika left with only two bodyguards and the driver in his official Land Cruiser Jeep to go to the Police Station.

Night had now fallen in Bulungu. The Ville area at night resembled Kinshasa, the Zairian capital, due to the presence of electricity. The only difference was the noise that came from the generators of electricity that they referred to as 'Groupe Electro-Gen'. After a few discussions between the neighbours and the Prosecutor the identity of Dada's father became clear to most of them. They were surprised to hear that he had a son living in Bulungu and in what they referred to as very difficult conditions.

A French freelance investigator journalist and novelist of international reputation, Rosemarie Baude, the wife of a French businessman, Francois Baude, was in the Judge's house at the time and claimed she knew Dada's father personally. "I heard him talking on the radio here and on French Television before," she said. "I was surprised to meet him personally." To a question put by one of the neighbours who was being curious, she answered: "Yes, in Paris, and he was alone," and she continued after the next question: "Last January, when my husband and I were in Paris. We went to meet my agent in the foyer of an hotel in Paris called George V. Isn't that true, Francois?"

"Yes," answered her husband, in a manner that suggested this was not the place for talking about their private lives—but that did not stop her talking.

"After my agent left, when I was still sitting there with my husband, guess who we saw sitting next to us reading a French newspaper? The Ambassador Tshienda himself! We introduced ourselves. I asked him if he could give me an interview in the near future, but I was surprised when he told me we could have one right then. So I gave him an informal interview. We talked about everything! He made his views clear to me regarding the so-called 'oil dollar'. The interview was fun. He told us he would like to invite us to spend a weekend with his entire family in his villa near Emmenbrucke in Switzerland, but unfortunately we were not able to make it. We did not even tell him that we also live in Zaire."

"What happened to the interview?" asked the Prosecutor. "Which magazine was it published in?"

"Oh," the woman gushed, "it was never published! My agent had an idea to convert the interview into a book which could be published around the world—that would be like the Ambassador's view of post-colonial international politics and the economy of the entire Continent. So I would have to interview him again and also get his consent. But after giving the manuscript to a few of his friends for critics, my agent called me and told me to kill the project! He advised me that one of his friends told him the man's life could be in danger if the project were to be accomplished. He told he didn't want to be a part of it—though I didn't ask much." She shook her head sadly, and continued, "I don't know if the manuscript has ever been in the wrong hands. I hope not." They were all quiet, listening to her. After a short while the Prosecutor told the people they could go to their houses so he would be able to organise the place. They could come back to spend the night, he said.

When the soldiers reached the Kabangu neighbourhood, in Gobary Road, to be precise, the place was dark because the neighbourhood did not have electricity. There were so many people on the streets with many small fires with people standing around them. They could tell where to start because they saw so many people gathered in one particular house. They jumped off their jeeps with the usual soldiers threatening slogans and also with their fully loaded guns. They did not speak the local language—not even French. They only spoke Lingala. So they had no time to talk to anyone. They just came to execute an order.

At first the people thought the soldiers were sent to prepare for the arrival of the officials of the town, but they got confused when the soldiers started arresting a few kids and put them into their jeeps. One woman presumed they were sent to get witnesses of the incident. She convinced the rest of the population to behave properly and also to bring the 'witnesses' so the soldiers could take them away. One young Protestant man who spoke a little Lingala came to them to strike up a conversation. Then he discovered the confusion. He tried to explain to them the version of events but they behaved like typical Presidential guards who only took orders from above. The Protestant man got angry and explained to the rest of the population what the soldiers were actually doing to their funeral. Bony's mother got angry like the rest of the people. She went straight up to one soldier who was still outside and ready to jump into the jeep so they could take off. She stood in front of him in a challenging manner while he had his gun towards her. Predictably, she started to shout at him so the rest of the people could join in. She aimed a barrage of verbal abuse at the soldier who did not understand what she was talking about. She even went further by trying to confiscate the gun from him.

Nobody could remember later on if it was an accident or a deliberate act. They just heard a loud gunshot and saw Bony's mother collapse. It seemed like time had frozen. It took the people few seconds to realise what had happened. Nobody was quite sure what to do at that moment. There was complete silence.

When the soldier who was involved in the incident realised what had happened, he jumped onto the jeep and they drove off. One courageous man approached with a piece of wood that had lights on top of it, close to Bony's mother where she was lying. He shook her many times. Then he looked at the people who were standing next to him and said quietly, "She's gone." They all shouted like a Church choir—"What!"—and crying followed.

No one at the funeral seemed to have any energy left to cause any further trouble. Even if they were willing to cause trouble, where would they begin? They needed to find a soft target first. Otherwise, Kabangu neighbourhood would be full of dead bodies. They knew what those soldiers were capable of doing. After a short time a few courageous young men, who realised they had nothing to lose, set off to go to the Police Station. One of them put it clearly to the rest of the people: "Tonight this town will become the Armageddon of Bandundu Province."

When they arrived inside the Police Station to meet the boys who supposedly killed Dada, the Judge said to Ms Betika, "What's wrong with those people outside the Police Station? They think I will be intimidated by their presence! I've already made up my mind. I know what I'm going to do with those boys." He shook his head. "They are just wasting their time. Once I say something, that's the way it's going to be! Those boys' parents will be sorry for what their children did."

When they entered the reception area of the Police Station, everybody who was sitting there got up as a sign of respect towards the authority. The head-policeman approached them. The Judge asked him, "Where are they?"

"I've separated them into two different cells," replied the head-policeman while leading them towards the cells. He also tried to inform the Judge and Ms Betika of Bony's mother's death, but the Judge showed little remorse for the woman's death. He didn't even ask for details of the incident. There was complete confusion at the Police Station, from the conversation to the protocol. For the few community leaders and the policemen who were there, the Judge had come to confront the boys and extract the truth regarding the death of Bony. But his disregard of Bony's mother death made them uncomfortable. As far as the Judge was concerned, he had come to meet those who had killed the Ambassador's son and would decide what to do with them.

When they reached the first door on their left, inside the corridor, the policeman who was with them opened the door so the Judge could see for himself. The Judge was the first to walk into the cell and he shouted angrily: "Qu'est ce qui se passe?" ("What's going on?"). The policeman looked at him with his eyes and mouth wide open, as if to say, "What are you talking about, I cannot grasp what you are implying. Can you elaborate, please." At the same time Ms Betika asked the judge, "What do you mean?", since she was still outside the cell and could not see what the Judge could.

Then the Judge realised what kind of mess they had created. But he was not the sort of person to apologise in public. He always let people make up their own minds as to whether he was sorry or not. At the end of the day, as he believed, he was for some reason the most powerful person in town. He always used to override the Mayor of the town in giving orders to people. This time he also kept the Mayor in the dark. The people of Bulungu didn't like him for his arrogance but they had no other choice but to deal with him.

While Ms Betika was still outside the cell, the Judge turned back towards her and said in a calm tone, "But…you told me the boy is dead…Look who is here."

"What?" replied Ms Betika, rushing in to see for herself.

"No, no, no!" interrupted the policeman. "He's the one who is accused of killing his friend by pushing him in the river, so he could be captured by the crocodile!"

"When?" asked a puzzled Ms Betika.

"This afternoon," said the policeman. "I was told it was an act of revenge."

Ms Betika felt dismayed and looked drawn. But it was not the same for the Judge, at least physically. Poor Dada at that particular time was sitting on a bench that was fastened to the wall of the cell.

"We also have, in the other cell, the boys who were present when the incident happened," the policeman said. "The soldiers have just brought them in."

But it was obvious that the presence of those boys in the Police Station was not as important to the Judge as the presence of Dada. So the Judge asked the policeman, "How did you get him here?"

"Someone came to tell us this evening that Mr. Masa's house was under attack by angry local young men because his son was involved in the killing of their relative," explained the policeman. "He is very lucky," the policeman continued, "that we were able to react before anything bad happened to him."

"Well, in that case," suggested the Judge, "bring all of them into your office so I can see what I will do to them." He added: "And also dispatch someone to my house to give the correct news."

At that time Ms Betika did not know if she should be happy because Dada was still alive or sad because of the accusation against him.

Once inside the office, they all sat in a semi-circle facing the Judge. The Judge had on his left the head-policeman and on his right a local community leader who was in the reception area when the Judge and Ms Betika came in. Ms Betika, who was reluctant to take part in the judgement of the boys, sat behind them.

The Judge asked one of the witness boys to tell the story of how it all started. They boy described everything up to the moment before the incident and stopped as he was instructed by the Judge. Then the Judge started asking them direct questions, one by one. "Who killed Bony and why?" He did not want to know *how* it happened but *who* did it and why.

They all answered without hesitation, "Dada, in revenge."

They were all puzzled when, asked about the incident, Dada himself answered, "Yes, I killed him in revenge."

No one spoke for a little while. Then the Judge asked the policeman for his opinion of what he, the judge, should do now. At the same time Ms Betika started to weep quietly. And the policeman surprised everyone inside the office by saying, while looking at the Judge directly in his eyes, "This boy did not kill his friend." At that the community leader cut him short by saying, "What do you mean, he did not kill him? He even admitted it himself!"

The Judge was quiet and everybody else didn't know what to say. The policeman said again, "In my eighteen years of experience in this Police Station, I could tell, by hearing what this boy had just said, that there are three main reasons that make him innocent of the crime."

They were all still calm and looking at him. He continued, "The first reason is, it is impossible for a ten-year-old boy to admit to a crime of this level to total strangers. Children always lie. They lie to get out of trouble. They agree with something to get the recognition or any benefit out of it. But there is no way a child will admit to any crime when he knows he could be punished. So he did not do it. The second reason is, children don't fight each other out of revenge. They fight, become friends and forget all about it. The third reason is there is no way a child could kill. I have been in Bulungu for a long time and I know children don't kill. The day children start to kill out of revenge will be the day Bulungu should receive a crown for being the most failed town in Zaire. I would also resign and accept all the responsibility. It's only adults who are capable of revenge killing—when they want to commit a crime they send some bad spirits to possess children, so the children get the blame. Those adult witches would do that to get away with it. And, looking at Dada, I don't see him looking like someone who is possessed by evil spirits. So he didn't do it."

The Judge did not know what to do and told Ms Betika to take Dada, to take the Peugeot 504 that belonged to the police, and put Dada in the boot so no one outside the Police Station would notice he was in the car. That way they could take Dada to his house, and Ms Betika could use the 'phony' to contact Dada's family to give them the news and to find out Mr. Masa's whereabouts.

Dada realised that at least someone was on his side. It was only when he was asked by the Judge to say if he had anything to add to what the policeman had said, that he surprised all of them again, first of all by starting to cry, and then by saying, "It's true, I didn't kill him."

The community leader immediately asked him a direct question: "If you didn't kill him, why did you say you did?"

"I don't know," Dada replied, and started to cry again. Then, in just a few minutes without anyone asking any question, Dada surprised everyone again by saying, "How could I kill Bony when he was my best friend? How could I kill someone who had taught me a lot in this town?"

The community leader was unconvinced. He asked him another question: "What could he teach you to make you not kill him?"

Dada did not know if he had answered that question, but it was necessary for him to do so. Then he said, "He told me about so many things that happened in this town that not many people knew about, like the attack on Papa Simon. I knew about it before it even happened."

Before he even finished the Judge banged on the table and shouted, "What is this? Is this a kind of joke or what?" Then he asked the policeman if he knew something about Papa Simon's attack. When the policeman answered "yes" the Judge became determined to find out more about the attack and told Dada to carry on. Then Dada told everything he knew about Papa Simon's attack, the conspiracy, and he gave the names of everyone who was involved and why. The Judge became intensely annoyed. Even the policeman, who didn't know what to do, started to say things that betrayed how fed up he was with himself for now knowing what was going on in the town. Dada, when he realised things were actually going his way, he kept revealing new disasters. He talked about a secret club that initiated children. Again, the Judge addressed the policeman: "I want some arrests made today of everyone involved in that guy's—whatever his name is—attack. All of them have to be sent to prison *tonight*. Not in the Police Station but in prison—tonight! So send people to get the Presidential Guard to make some immediate arrests."

No one knew what to say, even the community leader. So Ms Betika took Dada by his hand and they left the room. They passed through the reception, not saying good-bye to anyone. They went outside where a driver waited for them in the car park. The driver opened the boot of the car and put Dada inside. The people who were sitting in the reception area went to see Dada leaving, all under the impression that he had got away with the crime. They did not know what had happened. They got angry but they could not do anything. Ms Betika got into the car and they left the Police Station.

The people, who were outside the Police Station protesting against Dada, did not realize he had just left in the car. The rest of them inside the reception area all started leaving and muttering under their breaths when they realised they would never get justice. The Judge ordered the boys to leave with the community leader and said to them he didn't want to hear about their story anymore. He informed the policeman that he would make Ville a no-go area for the rest of the population, just for a short while, especially for those from the Kabangu area. He just wanted the policeman to know so he would not be surprised. He didn't ask his opinion but just informed him so he wouldn't be shocked when he saw the Ville full of soldiers. The Judge had connections with the army barrack, which was nearby, so he could arrange for many soldiers to guard the area.

When Ms Betika and Dada left, the Judge stayed behind. The Judge started telling the community leader who was still present a few things, then told him to leave as well as the boys. So the community leader left, but stopped at the reception with the boys to brief his friends about what had just happened and what they had concluded. The rest of the community leaders who were at the reception were angry about what the Judge had done. They expressed their unease regarding the Judge's attitude towards Bony's mother's death and the event. The conspiracy to kill Papa Simon was, as far as they were concerned, no more than a theory, and they were not prepared to accept the Judge's conclusive response and called it an excuse to set the boy free. They left the Police Station without saying good-bye to any policemen who were with them in the reception. Once they were outside the Police Station compound they informed the rest of the population who were there waiting to find out what would happen to Dada. They also became angry and started to throw some verbal abuse at Dada, although he had already gone. The most amazing thing was not how determined they had become in their willingness to challenge the authority, but the presence of some Protestant people in what everybody in the area considered as a Catholic problem. Their unity in action was spontaneous, something no one could ever have predicted. While they were still discussing what to do next after the failure of the authority to give them some kind of justice, one man raised his voice: "Quiet, quiet! Listen to me, all of you. We're not going to achieve anything by being here and shouting abuse at the boy. How can the authorities let him leave this place while they knew very well that we were still waiting here to find out what would happen to him? So let's go home and mourn for our beloved. There is nothing we can do now. They have money and weapons; we cannot fight them, so let's go home."

Instead of dispersing in different directions, they all took the same direction towards Bony's house. It happened as if they were being directed to go just to that one place.

When she reached the Judge's house, Ms Betika instructed the driver to wait outside the compound so she could go alone inside. "You could let the boy inside the car now," she concluded. Once inside the Judge's house, she spoke briefly about what had happened. She called the Prosecutor who was still waiting for his friends to come back, so they would know what to do. Ms Betika and the Prosecutor went outside to talk. Then she tried to convince him about the possibility of letting Dada spend the rest of the weekend at the Presidential Mansion. She was also thinking she might return to the Judge's house, to use the 'phony' to find a solution to Dada's problem. The Prosecutor agreed and told Ms Betika not to worry because he would send his bodyguard to call the Presidential Guards, using the 'phony', before she arrived there. Ms Betika did not even see the necessity of going back inside the house again, so she started to go towards the gate. The Prosecutor called her with all the politeness that she deserved, "S'il vous plait, s'il vous plait." She turned and walked back towards the Prosecutor who said, "I almost forgot, there is a young girl who is also spending a weekend in that house. She is called Tatiana. She's a very quiet girl. Her father is a personal advisor to the President and also the Chairman of the Zairian Bank of Development. I'm sure you've heard of him."

"What is she doing here alone?" asked a surprised Ms Betika before the Prosecutor even had time to finish his phrase properly.

"She's studying in one of the all-girl boarding schools near Kikwiti," replied the Prosecutor. "She spends most of her weekends in the Residence, unless the President is around."

"Does the President also come here on any unofficial visits?" asked Ms Betika.

"Oh, yes," replied the Prosecutor. "He loves this place. I don't know why he loves it, but it could be because it's the last place anyone would think he would be. He spends some of his time here when he wants to take time off from work."

"Okay, I think I have to go. I'll see you soon, because I'm coming back to use the phony to get in touch with Kinshasa. I would like this boy to leave Bulungu as soon as possible. There is no way he will be accepted here in this town again. Many people did not know who his father was, but now everyone knows. He was not even known in any neighbourhood besides Kabangu, but now everybody knows his real identity. They also think he killed his friend. Even yourself—can you really believe what they are believing? They must be stupid to believe what they have pushed themselves to believe. Since when was a ten year old kid able to kill someone? Let me put it in a different way—since your childhood, have you ever heard of a child killing another child out of revenge?"

"No," replied the Prosecutor, "but what do you personally think? Did he or did he not kill his friend?"

"I like following my intuition," replied Ms Betika.

"What is your intuition?" asked the Prosecutor.

"My intuition is that I shouldn't have to think of anything now. What I want to do is to get the boy out of here as soon as possible. If I can successfully get in touch with his parents or with Kinshasa tonight, then I will have to go to Kinshasa myself early tomorrow morning via Kikwiti. So I can get a seven o'clock plane. I will do my best to come back before six o'clock in the evening. I hope by then I will know what is to happen to the boy."

"Okay," said the Prosecutor. "I am not going home until you have succeeded in getting in touch with someone in Kinshasa. I could arrange a quick means of transportation to get you to Kikwiti. If you want to get there before seven in the morning, you have to leave tonight. Otherwise you won't get there by that time. There is a helicopter stationed at the Presidential Palace just for emergencies. I could arrange for it to take you to Kikwiti early in the morning if everything goes as planned. It is the same helicopter that the girl, Tatiana, uses between her boarding school and here every weekend."

With these words Ms Betika left for the Presidential Mansion. Before she got there the Prosecutor had already used the phony to announce her arrival so everything would be done as planned. Dada was given a bed to rest but he was not able to sleep. He couldn't believe what was happening to him. Being transported in a boot of a car was the last thing, he thought, that would ever happen to him. He could not believe he was still alive. But he was comforted when Ms Betika told him she was going to try and get in touch with his parents. When Ms Betika returned to the Judge's house, the Judge was already there. They went inside the phony station which was within the Judge's compound, near the garden. As usual, the Judge was in control of everything. He instructed the operator to send the message at the station, which was located inside the army barrack that surrounded the official Presidential Palace in Kinshasa. Soon there was a rapid flow of messages going back and forth and negotiations to try to locate someone who would volunteer to pass on the message to the Foreign Affairs Department, or to any official who could pass on the message to Dada's father personally.

They were delighted, after many security checks, to finally be told that the Ambassador had arrived back in Kinshasa that morning from Geneva where he had spent one week with some European official to negotiate certain agreements. Ms Betika was happy to find out that everything was going according to her plan. Although she was not able to speak to him personally, Ms Betika was nevertheless happy to be given an appointment to see him in his official house on Sunday morning before he flew back on the same day in the evening to Brussels where he would have to meet the President and catch his flight to New York.

After securing everything, Ms Betika went to her house. By the time she arrived there her houseboys had already finished their duties and left for the weekend. So she packed some things in her bag and then left for the Presidential Mansion where she would also have to spend the night in order to use the helicopter early in the morning.

Chapter 15

As planned, Ms Betika left early in the morning by helicopter for Kikwiti so she could catch the plane for Kinshasa. At that time Dada was still asleep. Although he couldn't sleep at night when they arrived, now even the noise of the helicopter couldn't wake him up. He had worried so much and it had made him mentally exhausted. Now he was able to sleep deeply. He was woken up much later by the sound of a piano coming from the next room to where he was sleeping. He was so tired with everything in life that he did not see the point of getting out of bed. He felt sick. He had a splitting headache, with pain all over his body. When he thought that the people in Kabangu might break into the house and pillage the place, he became momentarily overwhelmed with anxiety. He was well aware that some of the items he possessed could not be seen by anyone else. If someone got hold of it, he could become a lunatic. Also, if the existence of those items came to the attention of the people of Bulungu in general or Kabangu area in particular, they would think he had sacrificed his friend to increase his own power—by making his friend, Bony, his spiritual slave. He calmed down by convincing himself that he was a very lucky person and that nothing would happen to him—because, if something were to happen to him, he would have been killed by now. So he believed that he had a 'strong blood'—an expression commonly used in the Bulungu area and referred to people who cannot be 'envouter' (bewitched). It had been said that no one could cast a spell on a person who had strong blood because it would either bounce back to the one casting the spell or pass on to anyone nearby that had 'weak blood'. It will have its desired effect, but not on him. This kind of thinking made Dada stronger. He was able to get up from the bed because now he believed he would survive anything and nothing could ever happen to him or his family or anyone around him. He got up to go to the bathroom the housekeeper had shown him during the night when they arrived. He realised he had lost the appetite for luxury since he had been in Bulungu. Although those people had changed in their disposition towards him and were no longer kind to him, he still wanted to live with them, especially in the Kabangu area. He was so busy thinking about this that he didn't notice the music from the piano had stopped.

The young girl who was playing the piano had left the music room so she could go downstairs to the visitors' library to fetch a book for her daily reading. On her way back they both met in the corridor. Dada was surprised to see her.

"What are you doing here, Tatiana?" he asked.

"Oh," she smiled, "the person I was told is coming to spend a night here was you?"

"What did they say to you?" Dada asked, worried.

"I don't remember," said Tatiana. "I think they said someone was coming to spend the night here before going to Kinshasa."

"Oh, that's okay," answered Dada, relieved. "I was studying here, but I have to go to Kinshasa." He smiled because he considered Tatiana to be naive. He saw himself as an 'éclairé'. The term *éclairé* was used in Bulungu to refer to people who had been enlightened by any hidden knowledge. To recognise one another, they asked questions such as, "How well are your eyes?"—and if the person answered, "My third eye is now open," or if he simply said, "My third eye is open," then both would know that they were both *éclairé*. If the person who asked the question wished to know more he would probably ask something like where, when and how it had happened. With such questions he would expect to receive replies as to where and when the person's Master had given him or her the secret knowledge.

Although Bulungu was a town full of supernatural beliefs, not everyone really knew what was going on. When Dada realised that Tatiana did not know what had happened to him lately he no longer felt anxious about it. He realised that Tatiana did not appear concerned about what he was telling her. She simply told Dada she was going downstairs and that she would inform the housekeeper about him being awake so they could prepare breakfast for him.

Dada and Tatiana knew each other well, their families being relatively close. They had never been friends or played together before, but they had spent one summer together at Tatiana's family apartment in the 16th District in Paris.

After Dada had finished his breakfast, they both decided to sit on the balcony overlooking the River Kwilu. The view of the river was beautiful and the place was calm.

"Maybe that's why Tatiana's father preferred her to spend her weekends here," Dada thought to himself, "so she can read and practice the piano." For the pupils and teachers of the boarding school where Tatiana was studying, where she spent her weekends was a mystery. And for the staff at the Presidential Residence, it was also a mystery regarding the school she attended. They believed that Tatiana's father simply wanted to keep her contact with outsiders to a minimum.

Dada had taken a book with him but was not able to read, having drifted into sleep while Tatiana was reading her book.

When she reached the National Airport of Kikwiti, Ms Betika was able to get a plane for Kinshasa. It took her less than an hour to reach the International Airport of Ndjili in Kinshasa. A waiting helicopter took her to the 'Camp Tshatshi, the army barrack that surrounded the official Presidential Palace in the part of Kinshasa called 'Mont Ngaliema' overlooking the River Zaire. When she reached there, she was escorted by two soldiers to the nearby horse racing circuit where a car was waiting for her.

The car had dark windows. It was a type of Mercedes commonly referred to in Kinshasa as 'Trapese'. One of the soldiers opened the back door of the car to let Ms Betika in so they could drive off.

Back in Bulungu, while they were both sitting on the balcony, Tatiana was still reading her book while Dada slept. While he was still asleep, Dada had a dream that felt very real. It felt like his body was becoming rigid, immobile and also as though someone was holding him down. He could see everything clearly, to the extent that it felt like it wasn't a dream anymore but reality. When he looked in front of him he saw, near the balcony but suspended in space, a big disembodied human head screaming at him! The head had a lot of hair and a beard as well. He was surprised that although the head had no body attached to it, it was able to scream so loudly. The noise was so loud that it seemed the house would collapse. Dada, although still asleep, could think clearly. He couldn't understand what the big head was saying but he was scared to death. He thought he was going to die and someone had come to kill him. He convinced himself that the big head was going to capture and eat him. He was not able to contemplate what was happening or sit back and accept his fate. So he decided to run. He tried to move his hand, then he realised some sort of force was holding him down, preventing his hand from moving. He tried to scream but no sound came out of his mouth. He panicked, realising how serious the situation was. Once again he tried to scream for help but nothing happened. He started to struggle with the force to free himself, but his body remained immobile. He tried and tried again with no success.

After a short time, just when he was about to give up the struggle and accept his fate, he realised that he was free to move. He thought, "No time to waste!" He decided to run downstairs to get help from the soldiers who were there. When he got up from the chair and took two steps so he could run away, he glanced back to see what was happening to Tatiana. To his surprise, she was still reading her book. He could also see his own body asleep in the chair next to Tatiana with the book on his lap! Then he realised he was about to run away without his body—and in an instant he was back in his body and woke up.

He looked around him. Everything appeared normal as before. He became confused as to whether he had had a nightmare or whether it was actual reality. He looked at Tatiana and she gave him a big smile and asked, "Are you awake now?" He was so confused that he didn't answer. He got off the chair and walked to the edge of the balcony to try to make sense of what had happened. He leaned against the railings that surrounded the balcony. He looked at the trees that he had just seen collapsing and noticed nothing unusual. Even the River Kwilu seemed calm with no strange big creatures jumping out of it as he had just seen. Then he started to question whether what had just happened to him was a dream or not. He convinced himself that it was not a dream but reality and thought to himself, "This must be a warning. Someone is after me!" The thought of sleeping at night frightened him. He felt helpless. He did not know who to talk to or who to get help from.

In Kinshasa, the car that transported Ms Betika to Dada's family house stopped at the gate. The driver said, "That's the place you are going to." The other soldier got out of the car and opened the door for Ms Betika to leave. They drove off and left her alone in front of the gate where she expected someone to be waiting for her. She was surprised that there was no one at the gate, though it was open. She was able to walk into the compound with no one or any security member asking her any questions. She couldn't believe the lack of security. When she walked in, she was not able to see where the house was because there were so many trees surrounding the house. After a few minutes of walking along a path towards the house, a big mansion loomed ahead behind the trees. Even at the time she approached it, there was still no one available to stop her. She became concerned but did not really care. When she reached the house, she walked into the foyer. She noticed two civilians wearing dark suits. One of them was taking notes in his notepad. She could also see a half dozen men in soldiers' uniforms. They were all wearing sunglasses and standing with their guns in their hands. The civilians who were taking notes spoke to her before she even said anything: "Take that corridor and you will see the parents' living room on your second right." She said nothing and went where she was told. When she reached the living room she saw a young woman who looked like a nurse coining down the stairs wearing plastic gloves and something to cover her mouth and nose at the same time. Before she said anything, the young woman addressed her: "Thanks for coming early. The body is still in the bedroom. The ambulance crew and his private doctor are on their way. Please accept my deepest and sincere condolences."

Ms Betika, dumbfounded, was at a loss to understand what was happening, but kept her cool. In spite of her confusion she realized she had been mistaken as the person they were expecting. She decided she had to leave the house as quickly as possible, but not until she had seen the body the young girl was referring to. She went upstairs and had no difficulties finding the right room since it was the only one with the door open. When she entered the bedroom she did not waste her time contemplating the luxury around. She just went straight to the bed and noticed something that appeared to be a human body on the bed sheets. She lifted the sheets and saw a dead body of a man who had a facial resemblance to Dada. She noticed something odd about the body. The complexion of the dead man's face was a cross between pale and slightly greenish. She covered the body quickly and came back downstairs and decided to check the family portrait to identify the person. After looking at all the portraits that were there, she concluded that the person she had just seen dead was Dada's father! She became afraid and decided to leave. When she reached the foyer on her way back, she saw the nurse talking to one of the civilians and the nurse asked her, "Oh, are you going already?"

"No," she answered. "I'm going to tell my driver to go home because I'm going to be here for some time."

"Oh," intervened one of the civilians, "Let me send one of the soldiers to tell your driver. That's their job."

"Oh no," replied Ms Betika—for this was her excuse to enable her to leave—and she added: "I also have instructions to give him." Then she left with no further problem. She was well aware how big Kinshasa was and decided not to waste time trying to locate Mr. Masa.

CHAPTER 16
▼

After leaving Dada' house, Ms Betika took a taxi to go back to the airport so she could connect with her flight for Kikwiti. She was disappointed when a security man told her the next flight for Kikwiti was in the evening. "But if you are in a hurry," said a young woman who was selling tickets, "you can talk to the Priest who is sitting inside the VIP lounge. He's waiting for a private plane. The plane is going to Kikwiti and he is the only passenger." Accordingly, Ms Betika went to talk to the Priest, who introduced himself as Father Jean-Benoit, and was delighted when he agreed to help her.

During their conversation Ms Betika realised that Father Jean-Benoit was a headmaster of a Jesuit boarding school somewhere in Bandundu Province near the town of Kikwiti. She saw Father Jean-Benoit as the solution to her problem. She explained Dada's case to him. She was delighted to find out that he was favourable to the idea of Dada schooling in his boarding school. For Dada to be accepted, the Priest explained, he would have to be classified as an orphan. Ms Betika had no alternative but to accept the offer. She thought the situation would be just for a short while before she got in touch with either Mr. Masa or Dada's mother when she returned from America for the funeral.

Ms Betika had yet another reason to be pleased, since the boarding school that Dada would join was not listed anywhere—not on any official list of schools—and produced the best students and well-groomed adults. Some people considered such schools exclusive, and any members of staff would be hard pressed to prove the contrary.

When they reached the airport of Kikwiti, Ms Betika arranged with the Priest to use his contact to provide a jeep with dark windows to wait at the Bulungu parking lodge, 'Barriere', in the late afternoon. She would send a telegram to the Judge to send a car to pick Dada up in 'Residence' and take him to Barriere where the jeep would be waiting to take him to Kikwiti. When Dada arrived in Kikwiti, the Priest would have another jeep waiting for him at a designated location to be taken to the boarding school. As planned, Ms Betika would come to Bulungu as if she knew nothing; and, after a week, she would be picked up at another designated place in Kikwiti, at a mutually agreed time, so she could go to Dada' new school. The Priest sensed Ms Betika's anxiety and patiently reassured her: "Don't worry, I will get the boy's details when we meet next weekend." He went on to explain that if she managed to get in touch with either Mr. Masa or the boy's family, she would be allowed to pass on the school address.

Later on in the afternoon, after the Priest had left, and when she was still in the Police Station of Kikwiti town centre, Ms Betika received the telegram from the Judge that she had been expecting.

The Judge acknowledged having received her message and urged her, for security purposes, to use the phony to confirm everything to the Residence. She was not surprised, because she guessed that was the way things should be conducted at the Presidential Residence.

It was an easy task to do for Ms Betika. But the person on the other side of the line was too curious. The Judge did not ask her any questions because he assumed everything was fine.

Ms Betika thought it would be appropriate for her to pass on the news face to face. She was well aware of the secrecy or, as they called it themselves, privacy, which surrounded the elites of the regime. She did not need to rush to spread the news because she believed it could take forty-eight hours before the public was told anything regarding the Ambassador. She suspected the news on the national television might break as: "The Ambassador Tshienda has had a heart attack and has been transported to Switzerland for treatment." His personal doctor would probably say it was just a minor incident and he would recover soon. The body could even be send to Europe—in other words, when the person was already dead. Then they could simply say he had another attack. That's why Ms Betika took her time.

After a while, talking to the operator who was very persistent in wanting to know more, Ms Betika gave in. She said to him, "What I am about to tell you is classified. Do not tell anyone if you don't want any problems"—and then she told him everything.

After their conversation, the man ran inside the house to tell one of his friends. It was only when his friend put his questions, asked in a surprised tone, that everything turned blue! "Which boy…?" he said. "The same one who came yesterday night…? Ah! The poor boy…I don't know how this spoilt boy can survive as an…So, when did his father die?"

Little did they know, Tatiana was walking in the upstairs corridor and could hear them. She heard them clearly. She started to scream and ran towards Dada who was still sitting on the balcony.

When Dada heard Tatiana scream, he jumped up to go to her rescue. They both met head on in the corridor near the balcony. Tatiana jumped on Dada. She hugged him tight. Dada asked her, "What's wrong, Tatiana? What's wrong with you?" He assumed she was in the grip of an evil spirit! He was surprised to hear her say, "You…your…your father is…. is…. is dead."

"What are you talking about?" he said, nonplussed.

Tatiana did not even finish what she was saying. Dada pushed her away. She was prevented from breaking her back thanks to two staff members of the 'Residence' and one soldier who rushed to help her. They managed to calm her. At the same time Dada, who might have been expected to be the one in hysterics, hastened to stand on the edge of the balcony overlooking the Kwilu River, saying nothing. One of the guards who was present immediately stood close to him to prevent any eventuality of his tumbling over, for Dada gave the impression of one about to end his life. To the guard's surprise, Dada stared at him and then appeared to be smiling and mumbling to himself, as if to say, "Everything is under control." The housekeeper on duty begged them to remain calm until the information had been properly verified. "No one," he added, "should take this news outside of this house." He looked at Dada who was still standing on the edge of the balcony and said to him, "We have had similar cases before. Some people enjoy using death as an excuse to get favours from us. If you look at if from their point of view then you'll understand. They know it's difficult for us to refuse favours to someone who has just lost a loved one." Hearing this, Dada left the edge of the balcony and went toward the rest of them. And he asked the housekeeper "Are you sure? Are you sure?" "Trust me my son" he replied, "your father is alive."

Ms Betika, who was still in Kikwiti, was able to secure a means of transportation for Dada but failed to secure one for herself. This time the helicopter was not available, so she decided to use public transport to get to Bulungu during the night when Dada had already left. She took a taxi to a district of Kikwiti called Nzinda, also known as Kikwiti 3, where she could get a lorry that would take her to Bulungu. Because she wanted to reach Bulungu at night, she decided to spend some time at the nearby market. Inside the market she overheard two men mention Bulungu so she engaged them in conversation. She was delighted when one of the men said, "We are going to pass Bulungu and we can give you a lift. Our Jeep is parked near S.A.S." S.A.S was a name of a building that housed a construction company.

When they reached the jeep, Ms Betika got in at the back and both of the men went in front. Everything happened so quickly, according to some eyewitnesses who were waiting for their transportation. "The driver should have been more careful," one man said to the European civil engineer who came from the S.A.S compound to take note of the accident before the place became overrun with people. Some of his colleagues had been trying to help open the jeep while others had gone inside the building to use the phony to inform the police and the missionary, who owned the jeep (they could see the name on the jeep). "I don't know what was wrong with him," he continued, "we all saw the way he failed to look properly when he was pulling onto the road so he could speed off. We knew something terrible was about to happen and we feel bad we were not able to prevent it. The way the big lorry was coming we all had the impression the driver had lost control. We had no time to shout to alert the jeep driver. I knew by the force of the impact that there would be no survivors inside the jeep."

"On which part did the impact occur?" asked the engineer.

"On the left end side of the jeep," replied to man. "I hate saying this, but regarding the people who were inside the jeep—the woman who is still alive should be taken to the hospital so she can die in dignity. And the men will have to be buried here and one will need to take either their hair or their nails to their families. Because, frankly, the state of their bodies would cause more sadness to theirs families than the death itself."

In Bulungu Dada had already been taken to Barriere by the Presidential guards and transferred to the jeep that came to collect him. After starting the engine the driver said to his co-driver, "Oh! Let me go and get some cigarettes." His co-driver said, "I'll come with you," and they went, leaving the engine running.

Dada, left alone in the car, began to reminisce about his arrival in the same parking lot such a short time ago. He became aware of the extent of the impact his arrival had on the people of Bulungu, especially those who lived in the Kabangu area. Prior to his arrival, he believed, Kabangu had been a peaceful though divided area. Faith was very important to the people, especially the young people. Now, ironically, they were all united—in hate against him!

Not far away, at that moment, were many people gathered at the funeral of Bony and his mother. They were deep in heated debates about almost everything. Some of them even ventured to point fingers at the establishment itself. They started talking of things like justice. Such talk was unheard of before. They were even talking of sending a delegation in Kinshasa to negotiate their participation in the decision-making process—a decision-making process of their town. They were no longer afraid of the regime. They wanted to see one of themselves in charge of the town.

The situation was serious. The way the inhabitants of Bulungu were becoming conscious of their society, waking up to their humanity, the Central Government in Kinshasa would have to do something to calm them down. If it didn't, Bulungu would become the birthplace of a people's rebellion against the regime. That was the last thing President Mobutu Sese Seko would want.

When the people began to praise Mulele, a former rebel leader, in public, the establishment had to take notice.

Whatever happened to Dada, he would never be forgotten in Bulungu for+-generations to come. From now on, they would take notice of the justice that had been denied to them. They came to realise that whatever Church they belonged to, it made no difference to the Central Government, which regarded each as the same.

While he was still alone inside the jeep, waiting for those who were to take him to Kikwiti, Dada was quite unaware of Ms Betika's accident. He was happy because he was leaving Bulungu and going to meet Ms Betika in Kikwiti. She would take him to Kinshasa so he would be able to join his family in America. The housekeeper had done a good job convincing him that his father was still alive, and Ms Betika had gone along with this—if only to get favours from them.

When he remembered again about his arrival in Bulungu in the same parking lodge, he smiled. He realised how just in a short time he had gone full circle. Although his departure was less glamorous compared to his arrival, he still believed he had done a complete circle and that it was time to leave the circumference, just like a tangent line.

This time he could see who had said something compared to when he came. He heard the co-driver with his mouth full asking his friend something, the driver answering "C'est le depart."

Those were the last words heard by the boy when the jeep that was to transport him out of Bulungu parking lodge called 'Barriere' started to leave.

He smiled as he remembered again the first words he heard when he arrived in Bulungu, which were "C'est l'arrivee." He linked the two phrases. He became amazed and said to himself, "C'est l'arrivee…. C'est le depart…".

"Well," he mused, still smiling to himself, "that has truly been a full circle." He paused to reflect. "Oh! Yes," he said, "Now it is time to go tangent."

THE END

About the Author

Frederick Kambemba Yamusangie was born and partly brought up in Zaire, now known as the Democratic Republic of Congo in Africa. He is the third born in a family of seven children. He has studied communication engineering at the University of Kent in Canterbury in England. He lives in Essex, United Kingdom. *Full Circle* is his debut novel.

0-595-28294-6

Printed in Great Britain
by Amazon